WEB WEAVER

Ann Coburn

WEB WEAVER

THE BODLEY HEAD
LONDON

First published 1997

1   3   5   7   9   10   8   6   4   2

© 1997 Ann Coburn

Ann Coburn has asserted her right under the
Copyright, Designs and Patents Act, 1988,
to be identified as the author of this work

First published in the United Kingdom 1997
by The Bodley Head Children's Books
Random House, 20 Vauxhall Bridge Road, London SW1V 2SA

Random House Australia (Pty) Limited
20 Alfred Street, Milsons Point, Sydney
New South Wales 2061, Australia

Random House New Zealand Limited
18 Poland Road, Glenfield
Auckland 10, New Zealand

Random House South Africa (Pty) Limited
Endulini, 5A Jubilee Road,
Parktown 2193, South Africa

Random House UK Limited Reg. No. 954009

A CIP catalogue record for this book
is available from the British Library

ISBN 0 370 32352 1

Papers used by Random House UK Ltd are natural,
recyclable products made from wood grown in sustainable
forests. The manufacturing processes conform to the
environmental regulations of the country of origin.

Typeset in Janson Text by
Palimpsest Book Production Limited,
Polmont, Stirlingshire

Printed in Great Britain by
Creative Print and Design (Wales), Ebbw Vale, Gwent

For my son, Alex,
with all my love

Author's Note

The Borderlands Sequence is set on the Eastern Border between England and Scotland. Cheildon is an imaginary place, made up from a mixture of different Border Hills. However, the wrecked planes, the peat hags, the ruined bothies and the danger are all real.

'Oh, what a tangled web we weave,
when first we practise to deceive.'

Sir Walter Scott

1

'Time's up,' said Frankie.

'One more minute,' said her father, picking up a brass ship's compass.

'Dad! You've been saying that for the past fifty minutes!'

'Man, this guy was some traveller,' muttered Frankie's father, moving on to an old leather map case.

'Which guy?' asked Frankie.

'The guy who used to own this house,' said her father. 'Back in eighteen hundred and something. He travelled all over the world collecting stuff.'

Frankie stared at the map case as her father stroked the leather cover. It moved under his hand like –

'– skin,' said Frankie.

'What?'

'The leather. It's like skin.'

Her father laughed. 'Yeah, well, that's because it *is* skin. That's what leather is.'

Frankie swallowed and her throat clicked loudly. The leather was pale and wrinkled. It made her think of old Mrs Hardy, who lived in the apartment next to theirs back in San Francisco.

1

'What – what sort of skin?' asked Frankie.

'Uh, pigskin, at a guess,' said her father. 'Something like that.'

'Something like . . .' repeated Frankie. Her father opened up the map case and the leather creased into folds just like the skin under Mrs Hardy's chin. Hurriedly, Frankie turned away, rubbing at her arms.

The map case was not the first thing to bring her out in goose-bumps. The long, high-ceilinged room was stacked high with oddities, each one tied with a white label. People were shuffling up and down the dim, dusty aisles between the piles of stuff, stopping to peer at labels and mark lot numbers in their catalogues. There was to be an auction that afternoon.

Frankie shook her head. She could not imagine anyone buying some of the things she had seen. Who would want a stuffed python with one eye missing and scales like old, yellow toe-nails? Or a hollowed-out elephant's foot with a potted plant stuck in it? Who could even think of settling in for a relaxing soak in a bath-tub shaped like a coffin? The whole place gave her the creeps and the worst of it was, they weren't even supposed to be there. 'Country House Auction', the sign had read and her dad had veered off the Edinburgh road without even asking her first.

OK. Great, she thought. So I'm spending my birthday weekend stuck in a big old house full of . . . dead things. Frankie shuddered.

'Cold?' asked her father.

Frankie scowled. 'Dad, we're in the Scottish Borders. In January. Sure I'm cold. I'm always cold.' Back home in California they would all be dressed in T-shirts and shorts, cruising the sunny sidewalks beside the sparking blue sea. A wave of home-sickness washed over Frankie and her scowl deepened.

'Hey, this is my birthday weekend, right? We're supposed to be going to the mall to buy me a camcorder, right?'

'Shopping centre,' said her father, bending for a closer look at the charts inside the map case. 'They don't say mall over here.'

'Whatever,' sighed Frankie, tugging at his arm. 'Let's get out of this dump.'

'Frankie Madigan, you have no sense of history. Look at your friends. They're really getting into it.'

Frankie looked. David was strolling around the room with his hands clasped behind his back, stopping every now and then to consult his catalogue as though he was a serious buyer. He looked the part, too, thought Frankie. Smart, clean and polished with his thick fair hair neatly combed. Frankie grinned. She had never seen David look untidy in all the four months she had known him. Once again, the urge to ruffle his calm surface grew strong in her. Frankie took a step towards him, then made herself stop.

Alice was the next one Frankie spotted. She was sitting cross-legged beside a box of old photographic prints. Her long black hair traced patterns on the dusty floor as she bent forward over the framed photograph in her lap. Her knees stuck out sharply

3

on each side and already her green trousers were mottled with dirt. Frankie sighed. The trousers had been bad enough when they were clean. She hardly dared to imagine how Alice would look by the time they arrived at the mall.

Just then Alice raised her head, caught Frankie's stare and gave her a dazzling smile. Instantly, Frankie was taken back to her first night at the photography club. She had made a grand entrance, sweeping in on her roller blades to hide her nerves, and everyone had stared as though she had three heads. Everyone except Alice. Alice had looked up and given her that same, dazzling smile. They had been friends ever since.

Frankie winked at Alice, forgetting her irritation with the trousers, then set off to look for the last member of their group.

Michael was tucked away in a quiet corner of the room and did not notice Frankie as she peered round a tall bookcase. He had found a collection of fossils, housed in a miniature rosewood chest of drawers. The top drawer was open, showing the blue velvet lining. Frankie could see a neat row of fossils, each nestling in a specially made hollow.

Michael's grey eyes were dreamy as he traced the ridges of an ancient shell with his fingers. Frankie watched his calm face for a few seconds, knowing that as soon as she spoke to him, his usual worried expression would return and his shoulders would hunch up until they were practically touching his ears. Thanks to his stupid, horrible dad, she thought, as she eased back round to the other side of the book-case. Thanks to his stupid, horrible dad spending years and years picking on him until he can't even move without asking somebody first.

Frankie turned to look back at her own father as he bent over the map case. He wasn't so bad, compared to some.

'OK,' she called, tapping her watch. 'You can have thirty more minutes. Then we are going to Edinburgh! Deal?'

Her father raised his hand in acknowledgement. Satisfied, Frankie set off to explore the house.

'Where are you going?' asked David, strolling up behind Frankie as she stood in the big square entrance hall.

'Don't know yet. I'm mooching.'

'Hang on,' said David, hurrying back into the dead python room. 'I'll get the others.'

Frankie moved further into the entrance hall and looked around. The doorway directly opposite opened on to another long, high-ceilinged room, crammed full of auction goods.

'Bo-ring,' muttered Frankie, turning away from the door. She walked over to the staircase which swept in such a tempting curve up to the first floor, but a tasselled rope was tied across the bottom. Frankie sighed and turned her back on the stairs.

The polished marble floor of the entrance hall stretched out in front of her. It looked so smooth and inviting that Frankie slipped off her boots and launched herself across it in her socks. She slid nearly to the front door before coming to a gentle stop.

Frankie grinned and decided to go for a faster second attempt, using the doormat as a launch pad. She took a good run-in and shot across the marble at high speed. As the stairs loomed up in front of her, Frankie realised she was not going to stop in time. She bent her knees and forced her body into a turn, just scraping the bannister rail as she passed.

'Yay!' cried Frankie, shooting off into the gloom under the stairs. She slammed into the wall at the back of the hall and twisted round to see how far she had travelled. Only then did she notice a third doorway, tucked away in the corner.

The door was open. The room beyond was full of shadows. Frankie peered into the shadows and picked out a darker, bulky shape. The shape was moving, back and forth, and as it moved, it let out a regular creaking groan.

Frankie hesitated, then stepped towards the doorway. The groaning stopped. Frankie stopped too, and stared at the shape. There was no movement at all. The shape was completely still, as though it was waiting. Frankie looked over her shoulder at the entrance hall, hoping to see the other three, but it was empty. She looked back to the doorway, where the dark shape crouched, still and silent. Frankie took another step.

The shape burst into life. It grew twice as tall. Its sides spread out and flapped like the wings of a bat. It lunged forward and Frankie covered her head with her arms. There was a loud bang and a blast of chilly air, then nothing.

Frankie kept her head covered until the echoes from the bang had spiralled away into the stairwell, then she lowered her arms and opened her eyes.

'Oh, yeah!' Frankie put her fists on her hips and scowled. 'That's friendly.'

The shape had slammed the door in her face.

'Looking for these?' said Alice, behind her.

Frankie turned to Alice, snatched the boots and hauled them on.

'What are you up to?' asked David.

'I was just about to go in there,' said Frankie, striding towards the door.

'Are you sure we're allowed?' asked Michael. 'I mean, the door's shut.'

'Yeah, well it was open until five seconds ago,' said Frankie, grasping the handle. She gave the door a hefty shove and stood back. Nothing flew out at her. An empty rocking chair faced the doorway, groaning softly as it tipped back and forth.

'It must have been a person,' muttered Frankie, stepping into the room and looking around. Full-length velvet curtains were drawn across the window, which explained the lack of light.

'What was a person?'

'Someone slammed the door on me just now, when I tried to come in. A woman,' added Frankie, remembering how the clothes had swirled and flapped.

'Got a bit of a fright, did you?' grinned David, pushing past Frankie. 'Well, she's gone, whoever she was. Nothing in this room but more lots for the auction.'

'OK, so why didn't she want me in here, if it's only auction stuff? A-and where has she gone?' asked Frankie. But the others had already disappeared into the depths of the room. Frankie stepped after them, then stumbled to a halt. Her eyes grew wide and her hands clenched into fists. Something was standing behind the open door. She could *feel* it, nudging at her mind.

'Guys?' she whispered, her throat suddenly dry. The back of her neck prickled. Slowly, she moved her head around until she could see the space behind the door from the corner of her eye. There *was* something crouching there, but it was not the woman who had slammed the door. It was black, with long, spindly legs angling out from a creased and bloated abdomen. It was watching her with one bright eye.

Frankie became very still. She dared not turn away but she was too frightened to take a closer look. The thing behind the door seemed to be a spider, but it was as tall as she was. Frankie felt the blood thunder through her veins. She stared from the corner of her eye, unblinking, and the single eye stared back.

'Are you all right?' asked Alice, at her shoulder.

Frankie reached out and grabbed Alice by the arm. 'Look! Behind the door . . .'

Alice looked and her eyes widened. 'Hey!' she said, breaking into a smile. 'That is beautiful.'

'What?' Frankie turned on her heel and saw an

old tripod camera, balanced on three spindly wooden legs. The gleaming brass lens cap winked at her.

Alice walked around the camera, studying the black leather concertina that formed the casing. 'All black and leggy, isn't it?' she said. 'Like a spider.'

'Don't be stupid,' said Frankie, wiping the sweat from her top lip. She moved up to the camera, reached out and removed the lens cap. The dark lens glinted at her. Frankie leaned forward and stared into it, seeing her own face twist and distort in the curved glass. Again she felt something nudging at her mind. There were secrets in there, secrets she could have . . .

'David! Michael! Come and see this!' called Alice.

'No!' said Frankie, straightening up and glaring at the boys as they arrived. She moved in front of the camera and spread her arms. 'I want this. This is mine.'

A hollow rattling filled the room. They all turned to see one of the velvet curtains dancing towards the windowframe. The curtain rings clattered along to the end of the pole and light flooded into the room. A woman stood silhouetted in the window.

'You can't have it,' said the woman.

They stared at her in shocked silence.

'You can't have it,' the woman repeated.

Frankie recovered first. She lifted her chin. 'Yes I can. It's in the auction.'

The woman strode into the room and the dark cardigan draped across her shoulders floated out around her. 'You can't. The camera is no good.'

David straightened his shoulders, hoping no one had seen him go into a frightened crouch. 'You mean it doesn't work?' he said.

The woman turned her dark eyes on him and he swallowed.

'I mean exactly what I say. It is no good.' She pointed to the camera and a look of hatred crossed her face. 'That is a web weaver.'

2

'A web weaver?' whispered Michael, backing away from the thin, black legs of the tripod. 'Frankie? Maybe we should go?'

Frankie ignored him. She was glaring at the woman, refusing to be stared down. 'It's not your camera,' she insisted. 'It's in the auction. You can't stop me bidding for it if I want to.'

'And you do want to bid, don't you? Already, you want that camera so much it hurts.' The woman gazed sadly at Frankie. 'You can't bear the thought of anyone else even touching it, can you?'

'Hah! That is so crazy!' said Frankie, forcing a laugh.

'Is it?' The woman took a step towards the camera, then another. Frankie felt her muscles tensing. She glanced at the camera and swallowed. The woman reached out a hand towards the lens and Frankie clenched her fists, imagining how the woman's fingers would smudge the polished glass.

'Don't!' she gasped.

'See?' The woman drew back her hand. 'It's starting to work on you already –'

'Course it's not,' said David, as firmly as he could.

'Frankie didn't want to see the lens get all dirty. That's only natural. You're just trying to frighten us.'

The woman shook her head. 'You should leave now. Really, you should.'

'Can anyone join the party?'

Frankie turned to see her father strolling across the marble floor of the hallway towards the room. At least, he appeared to be strolling, but Alice was half-running beside him to keep up. His expression was mild and friendly, but his eyes were taking in Frankie's anxious face as the woman stood over her. Quickly, smoothly, he moved between them and Frankie sagged with relief.

Mr Madigan stretched out a hand. 'John Madigan, ma'am,' he said. 'I see you've already met my daughter.'

'We'll be all right now,' whispered Alice, slipping behind Mr Madigan to stand next to Frankie.

'Yeah, well, you didn't need to go running for my dad,' Frankie hissed. 'I was doing OK on my own.'

Quickly, she stepped up beside her father, pretending not to see Alice roll her eyes to the ceiling. Mr Madigan threw her a sideways glance.

'Frankie? Care to tell me what's going on?'

'I want to bid for that camera, Dad.'

Frankie pointed over her shoulder and Mr Madigan turned to look. His eyes widened with surprise.

'You want to what?'

'I want to buy it. For my birthday.'

'Oh, now, honey, those old cameras cost more than

you think. I don't think we can stretch to that as well as a camcorder –'

'No. Not as well as. I want that instead of a camcorder.'

Mr Madigan frowned. 'Hey, come on! Remember all those movies you're so desperate to make?'

'Not any more,' declared Frankie, but Mr Madigan was shaking his head.

'I don't think so. I know you. One week and you'll be completely bored with it.'

'Dad!' yelled Frankie. 'Will you listen? I want that camera –'

'Frankie.' Mr Madigan put up a warning hand. 'Don't start on me, OK? And I hope you haven't been behaving like this towards – um –' He turned to the woman and raised his eyebrows enquiringly.

'I'm Mrs Fraser,' said the woman, glancing at Frankie before turning to smile at Mr Madigan. 'And yes, your daughter has been quite rude to me.'

Frankie felt her eyes begin to smart at the unfairness of it all. 'But, Dad! You don't understand, I didn't start anything! She started on me!'

'It's true, Mr Madigan,' said David, stepping forward. 'She – Mrs Fraser – she tried to stop us from coming in here to look around. Then she told us we couldn't have the camera.'

'Couldn't?' said Mr Madigan, frowning.

'She said it was a – a web weaver,' whispered Michael.

'A what?'

'She was trying to frighten us, Mr Madigan,' said Alice. 'That's why I came to get you.'

'Uh huh.' Mr Madigan squared his shoulders and turned to face Mrs Fraser. His smile had disappeared. 'Were you trying to frighten them?'

Mrs Fraser pulled her cardigan tight about her. 'Mr Madigan, you mustn't let your daughter have that camera. It is part of a small ... special ... collection of items which were never meant for sale. I am – I was – the housekeeper here. I know the family would not have wanted that camera in the auction.'

Fascinated, Frankie leaned forward. 'What's special about it?' she asked.

Mrs Fraser gave Frankie a quick irritated glance, then looked back to Mr Madigan. She seemed uncomfortable, as though she knew he would not believe what she had to say next. 'The things in that collection are all more than they seem. They all have a strange – a bad – history. I'm warning you, that camera is trouble.'

A look of disgust crossed Mr Madigan's face. He folded his arms. 'So. You were trying to frighten them. A group of kids. Why? Do you want the camera for yourself? Is that it?'

'Mr Madigan,' began the housekeeper. 'I will admit I was trying to stop your daughter from bidding for the camera –'

'You deliberately scared a group of kids!'

Mrs Fraser jumped at the shouted interruption and took a step back, swallowing nervously, but Mr

Madigan only scowled down at the floor and let out a long breath. When he spoke again, his voice was back under control.

'Mrs Fraser, if there is one thing I hate, it is a bully. Let me tell you now, the only way you can stop my daughter from buying that camera is to be at the auction this afternoon and to bid against her. Come on, kids.'

Mr Madigan turned and strode from the room.

'Wow!' breathed Alice, following at his heels with David close behind. Frankie allowed herself a triumphant grin in Mrs Fraser's direction before she left too. Michael was the only one to linger, with a troubled look on his face. Mrs Fraser turned her dark eyes on him for a moment, then she shrugged.

'I tried,' she said.

Michael nodded, waiting.

'It might be all right,' said Mrs Fraser. 'But, if you ever need to talk to me, I live at the lodge down by the gates. I'm in most days, especially this time of year.'

Michael nodded again, satisfied, and hurried away to catch up with the others. When he was out of sight, Mrs Fraser stood frowning for a moment, then she walked over to a glass-fronted bookcase and opened it with a key from the ring at her waist. She selected a small, battered book with a faded red cover and carried it over to the camera.

A rectangular mahogany box was nestled beneath the tripod legs. Mrs Fraser released the brass fastening hook and raised the lid to reveal a neat row of narrow, black cases. She reached down to the back of the box and squashed the little book in behind the last case. Gently, she touched the book with one finger before closing the box again.

'It might be all right,' she murmured. 'It might . . .'

The crack of the auctioneer's gavel was loud in the quiet room.

'Sold! To the young lady in the sunshine yellow top! At a knock-down price, I might add,' he muttered, below the rising hum of voices.

'All right!' crowed Frankie, racing down to the front of the room with her father. All around her, people were peering at their catalogues and asking one another how they had missed such a treasure at the viewing. Alice looked over to David and smiled.

'Seems like Mrs Fraser did an excellent job of keeping that camera hidden,' she said.

'Yeah, until our Frankie came along,' laughed David.

At the front of the room, Frankie's father put away his wallet and hoisted the tripod up on to his shoulder. David's eyes shone as he watched the camera move towards them. 'I can't wait to see what kind of photographs we get from it, can you, Michael?'

Michael was watching Frankie as she scurried along beside Mr Madigan. Her face was a tight little mask and she never took her eyes off the camera as it was carried high above her head.

'Do you really think she's going to let you near that thing?' he asked.

'Who, Frankie? Of course she will. Frankie always shares everything. She's good like that.'

Michael shrugged and switched his gaze to the dipping, swaying camera. The brass lens casing glinted as it panned the room, swivelling back and forth like a big, round eye. Michael shuddered as it turned on him and his hand crept to his pocket. He pulled out a bunch of keys and began sliding them through his fingers, one by one.

Alice frowned. The key-counting was an old habit of Michael's. It was a comfort ritual, something which calmed him when he was feeling bad. Usually, a run-in with his dad triggered the key-counting. Today it was the camera. Alice looked at Michael's worried face and nudged David.

'Look at him,' she whispered.

David nodded. 'I know what he's fretting about.'

'What?' asked Alice.

'All that web weaver nonsense. He's taking it seriously. Now isn't that just like Michael?'

Alice sniggered and firmly squashed down the frightened little voice at the back of her own mind; the one that kept asking, but what if it's true?

3

'I still don't get it,' Alice insisted, gazing at the film posters which covered the walls of Frankie's room. 'Why? Why did you come home with that thing when you've been talking about getting a camcorder for ages?'

Frankie turned to Alice with an impatient sigh, then stopped and gazed at the posters too. A bewildered expression crossed her face. 'Why . . . ?' She twisted back to the camera and her excited smile returned. 'Look at it, Alice! It's – it's beautiful! I mean, anyone can have a camcorder, right?'

'Right,' agreed David, bending to open the mahogany box.

'Wrong,' said Alice, with a touch of irritation. 'Actually, no, not everyone can have a camcorder –'

'OK, OK,' said Frankie. 'What I meant was, camcorders are easy to buy, if you've got the money. But how many people do you know with a genuine Victorian tripod camera? Besides, I can always sell it if I change my mind, can't I? So, I'll be able to have some fun with this and then buy a camcorder!'

Alice shrugged.

'Right,' said Frankie. 'Let's figure out how it works.

Come on, Michael, you're supposed to be the clever one around here.'

David and Alice shared a look. 'Michael went home, Frankie,' said David.

'What?' Frankie stepped away from the camera and gazed around the room. 'I didn't hear him go.'

'He never came into the house. He said goodbye at the car when you were busy getting the camera up to your room. He wasn't feeling too good.'

'Oh. Um. What was wrong?'

David did not know how to answer that question, so he kept silent. Frankie turned to Alice.

'He was – scared, I think,' muttered Alice.

Frankie blinked, then shrugged. 'Scared? Of what?' she asked in an off-hand voice.

'Oh, don't pretend you've forgotten all that web weaver talk,' snapped Alice. 'You know what Michael's like about stuff like that. It's made him scared of the camera. He doesn't like being near it.'

'Aw, come on! He was probably just car sick,' cried Frankie.

Alice said nothing, remembering how Michael had hurried away without looking back.

'He – he is coming round tomorrow, though, isn't he?' asked Frankie. 'For my birthday? And you two?'

'Of course we will,' said David.

Frankie grinned. 'Good. Dad says I can do what I like, so long as I stay home. He's got something planned. A surprise. He seems pretty excited about it.'

'Oh, I know what these are,' said David, pulling one of the slim black cases from the mahogany box.

'What?' asked Frankie.

'I think it's a photographic plate,' said David. 'They used these before they had film.' He pulled at the side of the black case and a glass plate in a wooden frame slid out. 'Yes! I'm right! They'd slot this into the camera, see, and then they'd pull away the case to expose the plate –'

'– and then push the casing back when the shot was taken,' finished Frankie.

'But how would you get a photograph from a glass plate?' asked Alice.

'I guess they coated it with some sort of chemical emulsion, same as they do to film today,' said Frankie, looking questioningly at David.

'That's right. You know, we could take these plates out of the frames and put cut film in instead. It'd be a lot easier to use. I'll sort that for you, if you like.'

David slotted the case back into place, then leaned closer, peering at the back of the mahogany box. 'Look at this, crammed in here,' he said, tugging at the little book. He eased the book out and held it up, smoothing down the red cover. 'What do you think? Some sort of instructions for the camera?'

David started to open the book, but Frankie leapt forward and snatched it from him.

'Let me!'

Frankie flicked through the pages, her face intent. She stopped, frowned, then threw the book across the room. It skittered away under her bed and hit the wall with a dull thud. 'Stories,' she said in disgust. 'Just some kind of useless stories. I don't need them! I need to know how to work this camera – that's what I need!'

'Then why don't you ask me?' said David, simply.

Alice stared out of the window. David was still explaining the workings of early cameras to a spellbound Frankie and she was getting bored. She thought about leaving but it was already dark outside and the pavements glittered with frost under the street lights. Alice decided it looked too cold to walk home. She turned away from the window, kicked off her shoes and settled back on the bed.

She loved Frankie's room. It was huge, with two big bay windows and proper window seats. There was a walk-in cupboard full of clothes and Frankie even had her own bathroom. Best of all, as far as Alice was concerned, it was always T-shirt weather in Frankie's room because she was allowed to have the heating turned up as high as she liked.

Alice stretched out happily, sinking into the softness of Frankie's duvet. She would have drifted off to sleep but something kept stopping her. Something she had to find. Something important that would lie forgotten unless she searched it out . . .

Irritated, Alice sat up and tried to think. At first, she could only remember a dull thud, then suddenly the rest of the memory slotted into place. Alice saw the little book flying from Frankie's hand and skidding under the bed. That was it! With a smile,

21

she reached down beside the wall and felt along the floor until her fingers touched the soft cloth of the book cover.

Gently, she eased the book up through the narrow gap between the bed and the wall. It was still in one piece. Alice dusted off the front cover and her fingers brushed against a raised rectangle under the cloth. She opened the book and found a gilt-edged label stuck firmly inside the cover. A three-word question was written on the label in graceful, copperplate handwriting. Alice peered at the fading ink.

The greater truth?

The greater truth? What was that supposed to mean? Alice gave up on the label and turned to the title page. It read,

A CHILD'S BORDERLAND LEGENDS
TALES FROM THE TRUTH TELLER

Alice nodded without realising it. Carefully, she closed the book and slipped it into the inside pocket of her jacket. Only then, with the weight of the book pressing gently against her ribs, did she relax. She curled up on the duvet and let her mind drift away from the warmth of Frankie's room, out of the window and up into the dark sky. Outside, she imagined looking down on the buildings of the old town as they clustered around Frankie's house, their red pantiled roofs edged with a white lacing of frost. The houses were surrounded by the high, fortified town walls and beyond the walls, the river ran, pouring into the icy North Sea.

The river was special. It flowed through the Borderlands from the Western Hills to the East Coast, marking the boundary between England and Scotland. Alice traced the river out of town, under the Royal Border Bridge and deep into the Borderlands, all the way to its source inside the highest of the Western Hills.

This hill was called Cheildon and it was very old. It had once been an active volcano, heaving up out of the sea three hundred and eighty million years before the last Ice Age. Cheildon Hill was now many miles away from the sea, but fossilised fish and sea creatures still swam in its limestone sides. Seams of coal ran through it, marking the ghosts of forests where wolves once prowled.

Alice had climbed Cheildon with her dad the previous summer. It had been a cold, hostile place, even on a bright August day. She remembered the crash sites dotted across the shoulders of the hill, each displaying the rusting remains of a World War Two bomber. Two of the pilots had never been found and Alice imagined them resting quietly in the deep bogs which covered the top of Cheildon, protected from the wind which drove across the bare hillside.

There was no shelter on the hill, apart from a scattering of stone bothies where generations of shepherds had waited out winter storms. Alice could see a lone shepherd now, pushing his staff into snowdrifts to check for lost sheep as he picked his way towards one of the bothies. A heavy plaid was wrapped around his head and shoulders and he wore leggings of sheepskin, tied into place with leather thongs.

Suddenly the shepherd stopped, turned and looked straight at Alice. His eyes were the brightest blue in a lined and weather-beaten face. He leaned towards her and Alice realised that the dream had changed. She was no longer above the shepherd, but standing on the hillside in front of him.

She gasped and braced herself to run but the shepherd was nodding and smiling approvingly. He seemed to be very pleased with her. Alice smiled back, feeling ridiculously proud of herself.

She woke with a start as something soft and heavy landed on her face. The hill and the shepherd disappeared. She drew a shocked breath and her nose filled with dust.

'Wha – ?'

Alice opened her eyes. She saw velvet, plum coloured velvet.

'Wake up, smiler!' yelled Frankie.

Alice pushed the velvet off her face. 'What?'

'We've got work to do.'

'Go 'way,' said Alice, yanking the material back over her head.

'No, really,' laughed Frankie. 'We've only got half an hour before my dad takes you two home and

Davey's just had a brilliant idea for my birthday tomorrow.'

Alice sat up, suddenly interested. 'Great! I love planning parties.'

'Yeah, well, it's not exactly a party. More like an amazing all-day event.' Frankie grinned at David, who smiled back, modestly.

Alice sighed. 'Yes?' she prompted.

'OK,' began Frankie. 'We're going to turn my room into a Victorian photographer's studio –'

'– and we're going to take proper studio portraits of everyone who calls in to see Frankie tomorrow –'

'– yeah, and my bathroom's going to be the dark room –'

'– where we develop all the portraits –'

'– and it is going to be one amazing day!' finished Frankie.

'What do you think?' asked David.

'Brilliant!' laughed Alice, jumping up from the bed. Then her face fell. 'But I wish Michael was here.'

There was a silence. All three of them looked towards the camera, uncertainly. Suddenly, the light from Frankie's bedside lamp seemed too weak and dim for such a big room.

That camera is no good. It is a web weaver.

Alice shivered as she remembered the words of the dark-eyed housekeeper. *A web weaver . . .*

'Do you think we should?' she whispered, almost to herself.

'Should what?' asked David.

'Try to use it?'

'Oh, don't worry, we won't break it,' said Frankie, deliberately misunderstanding what Alice was getting at. 'They're really easy to use, these old cameras. Aren't they, Davey?'

'Um . . .'

David gave Alice a sideways glance. Frankie saw it and sprang across the room to flick on the main light.

'There,' she said, as all the shadows disappeared. 'Hey, come on, you guys! I mean I wish Michael was here, too. But –' Frankie stopped and moved in front of the camera to make David and Alice look at her. 'But this way, we get to surprise him!'

David blinked. 'That's true.' He turned to Alice and grinned. 'It'll be worth it just to see the look on his face.'

'All right, then,' said Alice. 'Let's get started. What do we need?'

'These,' said Frankie, dragging more velvet curtains from the bottom of her cupboard. 'And these.' She held up a hammer and a box full of tacks.

When Mr Madigan knocked on the bedroom door half an hour later, they had turned one of the window seats into a velvet-lined bower with a velvet canopy overhead.

'What do you think, Dad?' asked Frankie as Mr Madigan poked his head around the door. 'Does this look like a Victorian photographer's studio set to you?'

Mr Madigan stared at the transformed window seat. Alice held her breath, remembering the number of tacks they had banged into the window frame and walls. David gently nudged at a large flake of plaster with his toe until it was hidden behind the velvet. They were both imagining what their mums would have to say on the subject of hammers and bedroom walls.

But then, Frankie had no mum to tell her off for ruining the plasterwork. Frankie's mother was dead. They could still remember the awful moment when Frankie had blurted it out during a fierce argument with David, not long after her arrival in the town. David had been well on the way to hating Frankie, but for him, that moment had been a turning point. He began to work hard at putting up with her wild clothes and her arrogance and, gradually, they had become friends.

Frankie had never mentioned her mother again.

Mr Madigan was still staring at the window seat. He frowned, shook his head, then turned on his heel and left the room. 'Come out here,' he said to Frankie, over his shoulder.

Left alone, Alice and David exchanged frightened looks, but when Frankie reappeared carrying a small table, she was grinning happily. Mr Madigan followed her, cradling a potted plant with glossy green leaves. Together they arranged table and plant at one side of the window seat.

'There. Finishing touch,' smiled Mr Madigan.

'Neat!' yelled Frankie and she hugged her dad.

'OK,' said Mr Madigan, turning to Alice and David. 'Let's get you two home.'

'And don't forget to bring back all the developing stuff from Davey's house,' Frankie ordered.

'She'd make a good prison warden, don't you reckon?' asked Mr Madigan, as he headed down the stairs. Frankie sent a pillow flying after him and he ducked to avoid it without even looking round.

By the time Alice and David climbed into the back of Mr Madigan's car, they had forgotten all their worries about the camera. It was a cold, hard-edged night, with no room for shadowy imaginings. The sky was frosted with stars and the street was floodlit by a bright, round moon.

'See you tomorrow,' shouted Frankie from the front door and her voice rang out clearly on the sharp air.

'Back soon,' called Mr Madigan. 'And remember –'

'– Mrs Gregory's only next door if I need anything,' Frankie finished for him with an exaggerated sigh.

Mr Madigan blew a kiss to Frankie and climbed into the driver's seat. 'Seat belts on, guys,' he said as he started the engine. 'And by the way, how about telling me what the story is with young Michael? Has there been a bust-up?'

David turned from waving to Frankie through the back window. 'Oh, no. Nothing like that. You have to make allowances for Michael,' he said, exchanging a superior smile with Alice. 'He gets a bit silly, sometimes.'

'Meaning?'

'He frightens easily,' yawned Alice, conveniently

forgetting that she had not yet dared to touch the camera.

'So, the demon housekeeper got to him?' asked Mr Madigan.

'Yes. Crazy, isn't it?' giggled Alice, settling back into the soft upholstery.

On the doorstep, Frankie waved and waved as the car crept slowly down the icy road. She kept a grin fixed to her face while Mr Madigan steered cautiously around the corner but, as soon as the tail lights disappeared, her mouth snapped shut. Frankie scanned the street and her eyes were dark and clouded, like black ice.

When she was sure the car had gone, Frankie stepped inside the house and closed the door. Silently, she climbed the stairs and walked into her room without turning on the light. The camera crouched in the middle of the floor, black and silver in the moonlight.

Frankie picked up a cloth and began to rub hard at all the places where David had touched the camera when he was showing her how to use it. She did not stop polishing until she was sure she had scrubbed away every one of his fingerprints, then she stood back to admire the result.

The camera lens gleamed softly. Frankie leaned closer, then closer still, staring into the depths of the curving glass. The cloth fell from her hand. Around her the house sighed and settled for the night. Frost patterns began to grow on the windows. Downstairs the heating boiler clicked into life then, later, shut itself off, and still Frankie did not move. She and the camera leaned together, head to head, and it seemed that only one shadow stretched across the moonlit bedroom floor. A shadow with many long, thin legs and one bloated body.

4

'No, no, no, John! You haven't grasped it.' Ian
Elliot ran his big hands through his hair and shook
his head at Mr Madigan. 'In rugby, you're supposed
to hold the ball. You're allowed to! Here. I'll show
you.' He grabbed a parcel from the growing pile
of unopened presents in the corner of Frankie's
room and tucked it under his arm. 'See? You run
with it.'

Mr Madigan gave his friend a look of wide-
eyed innocence. 'But what about the hand ball
rule?'

'That's football, man! Football!' roared Ian. He
was a burly, red-haired ex-navy man and he roared
very loudly. All the other noise in the room came
to a sudden stop and, in the silence which followed,
Mr Madigan began to laugh. He had worked with
Ian Elliot on the Trident Oil survey boat for the past
four months and he had never yet failed to wind him
up when he wanted to.

'Gotcha,' he said, popping open a can of beer and
holding it out. 'Again.'

Ian took the beer with a rueful grin and everyone
else went back to their own conversations. Frankie's

31

room was full of people, all come to wish her a happy birthday. Mr and Mrs Turnbull from the bookshop were sitting on the bed chatting with Sally Ingram, the local poet. Rory and Heather, the two Turnbull children, were popping in and out of Frankie's walk-in cupboard, trying on all her brightest clothes. It seemed that most of Frankie's class at school were crammed into the corner by the far window seat, working their way through the cake and crisps and checking out her CD collection.

Slowly, the noise built up again. Only three people in the room were silent. Mrs Gregory from next door sat uncomfortably alone in the velvet-lined window seat, staring dubiously at the camera. Frankie hovered close to David as he helped her to set up for the first shot, and Michael stood beside the door, watching Frankie.

'So,' muttered David. 'You've checked that it's in focus?'

Frankie nodded, her face tense.

'And we've worked out the exposure time. OK then . . .' David opened the mahogany box and lifted out one of the plate cases. 'I've put cut film in here instead of the glass plate,' he said. 'So we shouldn't have any problems developing it – as long as that camera works.' He looked at Frankie.

'It'll work,' said Frankie.

'I'll time it for you,' said David. 'Ready to give it a go?'

Frankie nodded and he handed her the film case.

She took a deep breath and carefully slotted the case into the camera.

'Are you ready, Mrs Gregory?' called David. 'You'll need to keep still for a short while.'

'Let's get it over with,' said Mrs Gregory, smoothing down her dress.

Frankie reached out and grasped the edge of the plate casing. Around her, the room quietened as, one by one, everyone turned to watch.

'Now,' said David. Frankie pulled the casing and it slid back with a rasp, exposing the film inside the camera. She leaned forward, her head close to the camera, and stared intently at Mrs Gregory.

'OK. That's it,' said David. Frankie did not move.

'Frankie!' he snapped. 'Cover the film!'

Frankie jumped and quickly slid the casing back into the camera. A second later the hissing began.

Frankie heard it first, being the closest. She snatched her hand away from the camera and took a step back. Mrs Gregory heard it next. She froze halfway out of the window seat and stared fearfully at the camera lens as though she was looking into the barrel of a gun.

The hissing grew louder. 'What is that?' muttered David, moving towards the camera.

'Don't! Don't touch it!' cried Michael. Alice glanced over at him. He was standing with his back pressed against the bedroom door. His face was pinched and white. Alice marched up to Frankie and grabbed her by the arm.

'What's going on?' she demanded.

'What makes you think I know?' asked Frankie, giving Alice a look full of bewilderment. Alice stared into her eyes and saw that Frankie was telling the truth.

'Sorry,' she muttered, dropping Frankie's arm and backing off. Frankie shrugged and lowered her eyelids modestly so that only Michael saw the sideways glance she gave to the camera under her lashes. His sharp intake of breath was drowned by the loud hissing that filled the room.

David peered at the black concertina body of the camera. 'Is it air escaping?'

'It's not going to explode, is it?' asked Sally Ingram, edging away.

Little Rory Turnbull started to cry. 'Snake! Snake!' he sobbed, his face turning a brighter crimson than his Spiderman T-shirt.

'No, love. It's that camera,' said Mrs Turnbull, but Rory was too frightened to listen.

'Snake!' he cried, running into the cupboard and slamming the door.

'He's scared of snakes,' explained Mrs Turnbull, unnecessarily, knocking on the cupboard door and rattling the handle.

'Shhhh.' Alice held up her hand for quiet. The hissing was dying away. It had lasted only a few seconds, but in that short time a great tension had grown in the room. Now everyone held their breath as the awful noise came to a stop.

'Kettle's boiled,' said Ian Elliot into the silence. A smattering of relieved giggles broke the tension.

'OK,' said Frankie brightly, as she removed the film casing and slotted in a new one, 'who wants to go next?'

Rory Turnbull let out a wail from inside the cupboard.

'I think we'll pass on that,' said Mrs Turnbull hastily. 'Come on out, Rory. Time to go home. Happy birthday, Frankie.'

The Turnbulls weren't the only ones to leave. There was a general drift towards the door. Frankie's face fell, watching them go.

Ian Elliot was very fond of Frankie, although he would never have admitted it, preferring to pretend that he found her a dreadful nuisance. He caught sight of her stricken face and strode over to the window seat. 'I'll go next, menace,' he said.

'Just my luck to end up with you,' groaned Frankie, giving him a shining smile.

Sally Ingram had been about to leave, but she made a sudden turn in the doorway and headed back into the room. 'Then me,' she said, smiling at Ian.

Alice nudged David and hid a smile behind her hand. Everyone knew that Sally was in love with Ian Elliot.

'That's the spirit, lass!' said Ian, and Sally's face glowed pink. 'We're not bothered by hissing cameras, are we? Come on then. I don't want to keep you waiting. You go first, then you can get off home for your tea.'

'Maybe it won't do it again,' said Michael shakily,

35

as a disappointed Sally took Ian's place in the window seat. 'Maybe it was just, you know, warming up.'

But the sinister hissing did not stop. The camera made the same unsettling noise when each new shot was finished. After the third time, everyone except Frankie was staring at the tripod with undisguised dislike.

'Don't look at it like that!' said Frankie, moving in front of the camera protectively. 'It's only a noise!'

'But how does it do it?' David was mystified. 'It's not as though there are any moving parts in the thing to make a noise like that.'

'Come on, Dad,' said Frankie. 'Take a seat in my studio and let's see what happens this time.'

Mr Madigan held up his hands and shook his head. 'Sorry. I've got to go.'

'Where?'

'To collect your birthday surprise. Remember?'

'Oh. That,' said Frankie, turning back to the camera.

'I think we should develop these shots first before you take any more,' said David, holding up the three slim black cases. 'That hissing could mean the camera's not working properly. We could be getting nothing at all, and this cut film isn't cheap.'

'Good idea,' said Mr Madigan. 'That should keep you occupied until I get back. I'm going to be quite a while, kids, but Ian's staying with you.'

'Just don't expect any bedtime stories,' growled Ian. 'I'll be down below if you need me, getting to know that good malt whisky I spotted in your kitchen, John.'

The two men clattered down the stairs, leaving Frankie, David, Alice and Michael alone in the bedroom. There was a silence. Michael was still hovering by the door, keeping as far away from the camera as he could. Frankie was gazing greedily at the film cases in David's hand. Alice tried to think of something to say; then she frowned, realising what she was doing. She never normally had to think of things to say when the four of them were together. She usually had to fight to get a word in. What was going wrong?

'So,' said Alice. 'Um . . .' She sent David a pleading look.

'So,' said David. 'Developing. How many people do you reckon we can fit in your bathroom, Frankie?'

Frankie stepped forward and lightly lifted the cases from David's hand. 'Oh, no need for you guys to hang around,' she said. 'I can develop this lot on my own.'

'Hang on,' said David, moving in front of the bathroom door. 'Hang on a minute. Are you sure you can manage?'

'Aw, get out of here! You know I did that last lot of prints without any help –' Frankie stopped and made herself smile. 'You've been a good tutor, Davey. I'll be fine.'

She tried to slip past David into the bathroom, but he moved with her, blocking her way.

'Not cut film,' he said. 'You haven't developed cut film before. That's different.'

'Can't be that different.'

'Still, I'd better be there,' said David, with an edge to his voice.

Frankie scowled. 'Uh-huh. Well you can't. You can't be there.'

David pushed his hair off his forehead and gave Frankie a hurt, puzzled look. 'I don't get it,' he said. 'What is going on? It's not like you to be mean, Frankie. You've always shared everything. Come on. Don't shut me out. I spent hours turning that bathroom into a darkroom for you this morning, and I'm really interested to see how these shots come out.'

Sudden tears made Frankie's eyes glitter. She blinked hard and cleared her throat. 'It's my bathroom.'

'And it's my developing stuff,' said David, folding his arms and raising his eyebrows.

'Uh-huh,' said Frankie, straightening her shoulders. 'So, if you can't play, you're going to take your ball home. Is that the idea?'

'That's the idea,' said David.

David and Frankie glared at one another. 'You know, that is so childish,' said Frankie.

'Take it or leave it,' answered David, pushing open the bathroom door. Wordlessly, Frankie marched into the bathroom and David followed, closing the door firmly behind him.

'Phew!' said Alice, unclenching her hands. 'That was just like the old days, wasn't it?'

Michael slid down the wall until he was sitting on

the floor. Alice hurried across and sat down next to him. Close to, she could see that he was shaking.

'Michael.' Alice gently touched his arm. 'Michael. If the camera bothers you this much, why don't you just go home? Why stay if it makes you feel so bad?'

'I've got to stay!' blurted Michael. 'To look out for Frankie.'

'Look out for Frankie? Why?'

'Because nobody else will, that's why!' Michael pointed a shaking finger at the camera. 'Nobody else can see how that thing has got a hold on her. It has!' he insisted, seeing Alice start to shake her head.

'How?' asked Alice.

'I don't know,' said Michael, miserably. 'But it has. Frankie's not here any more.'

'Oh, now that is stupid –'

'Is it? Has she checked out your clothes today?'

'What?'

'Has she told you that –' Michael stopped to take a look at what Alice was wearing, '– that blue and brown don't go together?'

Alice looked down at her favourite shirt and jeans and opened her mouth to protest, but there was no stopping Michael now he had started to talk.

'Has she dragged you into her cupboard to tie scarves in your hair or try out some new eye stuff?'

'Well, no,' said Alice, beginning to understand what Michael was getting at.

'No,' said Michael. 'And she hasn't been marching

me around the room, telling me not to be so shy and introducing me to every single person, either. In fact, she hasn't talked to me at all,' he finished, looking down at his hands.

'Yeah, but then she's hardly talked to anyone today . . .' Alice trailed to a stop.

'Exactly. And look.' Michael nodded at the pile of unopened presents.

'You know what Frankie's like,' said Alice doubtfully, staring at the bright packages. 'She gets these crazes.'

'But look at those presents! How can she not open them? That's not natural. This thing with the camera, it's more than a craze, Alice.'

'Yes.' Alice nodded, finally accepting what Michael was saying. 'What can we do?'

'I don't know.'

Alice looked up at her jacket, hanging behind the door. 'Listen,' she said, clambering to her feet. 'Yesterday David found a little book in the camera box. Frankie threw it away but I picked it up and kept it. I don't know why, but I felt as though I ought to.' Alice fished the book out of the inside pocket of her jacket and handed it to Michael.

Michael opened the book. '*Tales from the Truth Teller*,' he read.

'Yes,' said Alice, sitting down again. 'And look, here, inside the cover.' She pointed to the book label with the copperplate writing. 'See that? "*The greater truth?*" Do you think . . . ? I mean, could this book be linked with the camera, somehow? Could it

40

– help?' Alice glanced warily at Michael, expecting him to laugh, but he nodded seriously.

'She might have put it in the box for us,' Michael said.

'Who, the housekeeper?'

'Yes.' He turned the page and pointed to a black and white line drawing. 'Look. The Truth Teller.'

Alice peered over Michael's shoulder and gasped. There he was, her shepherd, standing in the snow. There were the plaid, the sheepskin leggings and the long stick, all exactly the same. 'I dreamed about him last night,' she breathed. 'Just after I rescued the book. I dreamed I saw him on Cheildon Hill.'

'Well, I suppose if this was the last thing you looked at before you went to sleep –'

'But I didn't see that drawing! I only looked at the title page.' Alice gazed at the shepherd's face and smiled. 'He had bright blue eyes . . .'

There were a few lines of writing under the drawing. Michael put his finger to the page and began to read.

'"*I promise you one thing, reader. My tales will never deceive you, for I am the Truth Teller. My life is in these tales. Call them stories if you must, but remember, sometimes stories carry a greater truth within.*"'

'A greater truth!' cried Alice. 'That's what's written in the front.'

Michael grinned at Alice. There was some colour in his cheeks for the first time that day and he had stopped shaking. He held out the book to her. 'You start,' he said.

So, Alice began.

Frankie slouched against the bathroom door and glowered at the back of David's head as he worked on the prints. He hummed tunelessly as he moved methodically from one tray of chemicals to the next.

Careful, precise David. She wanted to scream. How could she ever have liked him? How could she ever have liked any of them? Frankie thought of timid, rabbity little Michael and dreamy, beanpole Alice. They made her want to spit!

'Nearly there now,' said David. 'I'm on to the final wash.'

Frankie leaned over the edge of the bath to peer at the prints, but it was difficult to see any detail in the dim red glow thrown out by the safe light. 'Man, you are so-o-o slow,' she sighed.

David turned to look at her over his shoulder. 'There is no way you could have done it as fast as me.'

'Fast!' Frankie laughed, then laughed again when she saw his expression. The stupid boy looked hurt!

'Do you want me to do this?' growled David.

'Yes!'

'Yes what?'

Frankie took a deep breath and made herself calm down. She was nearly there. Soon she would see all the secrets the camera was keeping. Then she would have no more need of David.

'Please,' she said. 'Yes please.'

'All right,' said David. He lifted the three prints

out of the rinsing water, one by one, and pegged them above the bath. 'You can turn the light on now. They're finished.'

Frankie yanked at the light cord, then, blinking fiercely in the sudden brightness, she whirled round to look at the prints. The overhead light hummed loudly in the silence which followed.

'Oh no,' said David.

5

Frankie gazed at the prints in horror. If she tried very hard, she could just about make out the figures of Mrs Gregory, Sally Ingram and Ian Elliot sitting in the window seat, but they were half-seen shapes, nothing more. Each print was defaced with white scrawls and scribbles, as though a bad graffiti artist had been let loose with an aerosol can.

'What have you done?' hissed Frankie.

'I don't understand it,' said David, looking from the prints to his developing equipment and back again.

'You messed it up!' shrieked Frankie, turning on him.

David jumped and backed away from her furious face. 'How could I have messed it up?' he pleaded. 'You were standing there watching me every step of the way. You know I did everything right.'

Frankie looked back to the prints, breathing hard. How could she see what the camera wanted to show her, when the images were so disfigured? She stopped and looked again at the scribbles. They were crude, but there was something deliberate about them, as though . . .

'You!' Frankie turned furiously on David and

slammed both hands into his chest, pushing him back against the door. 'You did it on purpose!'

'No way!' yelled David, but Frankie was not listening. She began to slap at him; hard, open-handed slaps which came so fast he could not dodge them all.

'You did it on purpose!' she cried. 'Because you're jealous!'

David curled away from Frankie, bringing both arms up over his head. He saw the doorhandle a few centimetres from his nose and made a grab for it. The door flew open and he stumbled out.

Frankie followed, still flailing at him, but David was over the first shock. He turned to face her and grabbed one wrist, then the other. 'Stop it!' he shouted, cuffing her hands together and holding her at arm's length.

'Jealous – of my camera – aren't you?' panted Frankie, trying to reach him with her feet.

David shot a glance over at Alice and Michael, who were sitting side by side on the carpet in stunned silence. 'Don't just sit there!'

Together they jumped up and ran to Frankie, each grabbing one of her arms. David stepped back. He looked very shaken.

'What on earth has happened?' asked Alice.

'Someone's scrawled all over the prints,' said Frankie in a hard, loud voice. 'Someone with prissy fair hair and a prissy little tight mouth and –'

'Right! I did not do anything to those prints. I wouldn't. I wouldn't do that, Frankie!'

Frankie stared at David in stony silence.

'I'm going to have a look at that camera,' said David, turning away.

'Don't you touch it!' yelled Frankie, breaking away from Alice and Michael.

'You can't get away with saying something that's not true, Frankie! I'm going to prove it wasn't me that mucked up your stupid prints. There's something wrong with that camera and I'm going to find out what it is. I won't hurt it. I'm just going to look.'

Frankie hesitated.

'Do you want to get good prints from it or not?' asked Alice.

'Course I do.'

'Then let David have a look.'

Frankie shrugged her shoulders and followed David over to the camera.

'And if I do find something,' said David grimly, 'you'd better be ready to say sorry.'

Frankie shrugged again, as though she did not really care.

'OK.' David peered at the camera. 'Where do we start?'

'Have a look at the leather concertina bit,' said Michael, hovering three feet away. 'There might be light getting into it somewhere.'

'Yes, and where light can get in, air can escape!' cried Alice. 'That might explain the hissing noise every time you push the film casing back into the camera.'

'Alice? Are you going to help?' asked David.

Alice made herself walk up to the camera. She reached out and touched the black leather, shuddering at the way it gave and moved under her fingers. Together they explored the folds and creases of the casing but they could not find a single crack or split. The leather was smooth and supple, showing no signs of age.

'Someone's looked after it,' said David.

'Or maybe no one wanted to use it much,' muttered Michael.

David moved on to the mahogany frame and noticed three deep intersecting cuts in the wood. 'Look at this! Someone's had a go at this with an axe or something. Must have been a long time ago. The wood's all the same colour now.'

'Lemme see that.' Frankie stroked the wood. 'Poor camera. They were trying to destroy it.'

'They didn't manage it though,' said Alice, running her hands around the frame. 'It's as solid as anything. Mahogany, see.'

Alice stopped as her hands found a rectangle of card stuck to the base of the frame. She crouched down on her heels and peered under the camera. 'Hey! Michael! Come and look at this!'

The excitement in her voice made Michael step close enough to peer under the camera. There was another three-word question on the card, in the same elegant, copperplate handwriting. It said,

Seeing is believing?

'That's the same –' began Alice, but Michael shook his head at her. For some reason he did not want her to mention the book. Quickly, Alice thought of something else to say. 'Um . . . strange. That's strange. What a funny thing to write.'

'Uh-huh,' muttered Frankie, without really listening. She was watching David as he checked for cracks around the camera lens.

'No,' he said, straightening up. 'There's no light getting in there except where it's supposed to. This camera is sealed tight. Beautifully put together. It's a pity we can't see inside.'

Frankie moved forward protectively. 'Why would you want to do that?'

'I'm wondering whether there's some sort of chemical in there. Acid maybe. Acid could mark film like that.'

'And acid would make a hissing noise while it was working,' said Michael.

'Yeah, well you can't see inside my camera,' said Frankie. 'Not without breaking it.'

'But look, if I loosened these screws here –'

'No! You just want to find something wrong with it. But there is nothing wrong with it, is there?' challenged Frankie.

'Not that I can see,' said David, calmly, fixing her with a steady stare.

'So. You did it. You vandalized my prints.'

'No.'

'You are one big liar, David Robson!'

Alice drew a sharp breath and shot a look at

Michael. They both knew there was one thing David would never put up with and that was being called a liar. David was always honest with everybody and he expected the same honesty in return.

David moved out from behind the camera and stood squarely in front of Frankie. He looked as though he was about to explode. Frankie put her hands on her hips and stood her ground. As they faced up to one another, Frankie's bedroom door swung open behind David.

'Don't you ever –' began David, but Frankie was no longer looking at him. She was staring over his shoulder and her eyes were wide with shock.

'Here's your surprise, honey,' said Mr Madigan.

David, Alice and Michael all turned to see what the surprise was. A small, very beautiful black woman stood in the doorway. She had the same slanting eyes as Frankie and the same bird-like bone structure. She was immaculately and expensively dressed in a jade green silk suit.

The woman gazed at Frankie and smiled, holding out her manicured hands. Frankie ran over to the woman and hugged her fiercely.

'Mom!' she choked.

'Happy birthday, Frances,' said the woman, gently easing free of Frankie's arms and smoothing down her suit.

'Don't call me Frances,' muttered Frankie, stepping back. 'No one's called me Frances for four months.'

'That's what I named you and that's what I'll call

you,' said the woman in a low, controlled voice, smiling over Frankie's head at Alice, David and Michael. All three of them stared back at her as though they had seen a ghost.

'I'm Samantha Madigan. You must be Alice, Michael and David. Frances has told me all about you.' Mrs Madigan stopped and studied their shocked faces. 'I seem to be a very – big – surprise,' she drawled. 'Has Frances mentioned me at all?'

'Only once,' said David, glowering at Frankie. 'She told us you were –'

'– too busy working to come over,' interrupted Frankie, giving David a look full of pleading.

David turned his back on Frankie. 'And she dares to call me a liar,' he said, under his breath.

Alice had stopped staring at Mrs Madigan and was staring at Frankie instead. How could she have told them her mother was dead?

'Frances is right. I was working too hard to make it over here for Christmas. I was real busy at Christmas. Do you know, we had nine freeway smashes in one day?'

'Freeway smashes?' said Michael faintly.

'Mom's a surgeon,' explained Frankie. 'She patches up people who've been in car crashes.'

'Oh, I see,' said Alice. 'Um, that's nice.'

'Well, Frances. You really have kept them in the dark, haven't you?' said Mrs Madigan. For a second, the hurt showed on her face, then she smoothed it away with a smile and stepped further into the room.

50

'What a lovely room. It's very large, isn't it? In fact,' added Mrs Madigan, glancing at the bathroom door and raising her eyebrows at her husband, 'in fact, you seem to have given her the master bedroom here.'

'Yeah, well.' Mr Madigan shrugged. 'She deserved it, didn't you, honey? Moving to a new place and settling in so well.' He glanced around, looking at all their faces and trying to figure out what was going wrong.

'My, my, my, Frances. You have been busy,' said Mrs Madigan, inspecting the velvet-lined window seat.

Frankie didn't answer. After her initial pleasure at seeing her mother, she seemed to have withdrawn into a sulk.

'Yes,' said Alice, stepping in to fill the silence. 'It's a studio set. For taking portraits.'

'Uh-huh. Lots of nails. In the wall,' said Mrs Madigan, again directing a look at her husband.

'Samantha,' he sighed, with a hint of irritation. Frankie's head came up. She looked from her mother to her father and bit her lip.

'OK,' said Mr Madigan into the lengthening silence. 'How about I get you a drink and show you where to freshen up?'

'Fine,' said Mrs Madigan. She moved over to Frankie and touched her cheek gently. 'It's good to see you, darling,' she said. Then she nodded pleasantly to the others and walked gracefully out of the room.

51

After one last worried look at Frankie, Mr Madigan followed his wife, closing the door behind him.

David, Alice and Michael all turned to stare at Frankie.

'Look, guys . . .'

'So. What lie is it next?' said David. 'Is it the she-made-a-miraculous-recovery lie? Or the she's-my-step-mother lie? Or maybe –'

'I would have told you, honestly –'

'Honestly!' roared David. 'Honestly? I don't know how you dare to use that word.'

Frankie flinched. 'I didn't know she was coming! If I'd known, I would have told you.'

'But why tell us she was dead in the first place?' asked Alice in a bewildered voice.

'Because it was easier than having to explain the whole thing about us being over here and her being over there.'

'No,' said David, shaking his head. 'No. You don't lie, just because it's easier. You don't tell your friends that your mother is dead just because it's easier!'

'Aw, come on! What difference has it made to you?'

'What difference? You are unbelievable,' snarled David. 'Do you know how sorry I felt for you? I've let you get away with so many crazy things since you told me your mum was dead.'

'So?'

'So we would've fallen out ages ago if it wasn't for your lie. We wouldn't be friends now, Frances, except for your lie!'

52

'Don't call me that!'

'I'm going,' said David, and he turned on his heel and walked out.

'Davey?' called Frankie, but there was no answer. Frankie spread her arms and gave Alice and Michael a look full of misery. She moved close to the camera, resting her hand gently on the top of it. As soon as she touched the gleaming mahogany, a strange thing happened. All the worry and confusion left her face, to be replaced with a blank, smooth expression. Michael watched the change and shuddered.

'OK, guys,' said Frankie. 'Party over, I think.'

'I – I'll stay – if you want to talk . . .' Alice offered, hesitantly.

'Naw, I don't think so,' yawned Frankie.

'Come on, Alice,' said Michael from the door. Alice walked towards him, then stopped to search the floor where they had been sitting earlier. Michael patted his pocket and she nodded, understanding.

'See you then,' said Alice.

'Yeah, well, I don't know about that. I may be busy, with my mom being over here.'

'Oh, right. Happy birthday then.'

'Whatever,' said Frankie, heading for the bathroom and closing the door behind her.

Alice felt her eyes fill with tears. 'Wh-what are we going to do, Michael?'

Michael turned up the collar of her jacket for her and wrapped her scarf warmly around her neck. 'Let's go to your place,' he said, patting his pocket. 'We need to finish reading this book. Then we need to talk to David.'

Frankie was only vaguely aware of the front door slamming behind Alice and Michael as she stared at the prints in the bathroom.

'Come on, come on! What is it?' she muttered, leaning closer. If she could only get past all the white scrawls. Frankie stopped and took a step back. Maybe she was looking at this the wrong way? She remembered her earlier feeling, about the marks being deliberate.

'OK. So, look at the whole thing together.'

Frankie concentrated on the first print she had taken, the one of Mrs Gregory, and suddenly everything became clear. The scrawls were not meant to hide the image; they were badly drawn additions, like a child with a felt-tip, drawing spectacles and moustaches on to faces in a newspaper.

With an excited grin, Frankie yanked the print from the drying line and rushed back to the main room. 'What are you telling me?' she asked the camera, holding the print under the overhead light. There was a mark shaped like a bowl with a stem beneath, drawn over Mrs Gregory's hand. By her other hand was a long container, growing narrower at the top. A whirl of white lines spun around her head, like the rings of Saturn, and crudely drawn stars were scattered amongst the lines. They made Mrs Gregory look like a cartoon drunk.

'A glass and a bottle!' crowed Frankie. 'That's it!

Mrs Gregory's a secret drinker!' She had overheard the adults in her street making remarks about cooking sherry and bottle-banks. Now the camera was telling her that their suspicions were right.

Frankie grinned as she stared at the evidence shown in the photograph. Her grin slipped slightly and she glanced at the camera uneasily as she thought of kind, generous Mrs Gregory sitting in her empty house with no one to talk to. Then her excitement returned and she hurried back to the bathroom as she remembered the other two prints waiting for her.

'OK. Let's see now . . .' Frankie held up the photograph of Sally Ingram. There were blunt-headed lines all over her clothes and her hands were joined together by two bracelets and a loop.

'Handcuffs,' breathed Frankie. 'And . . . arrows! A convict suit!'

She remembered how Emma Beresford had come into school one Monday just before Christmas with some gossip. Emma had been shopping in Edinburgh at the weekend and she claimed to have seen a woman who looked very like Sally being led away from a store by a policeman. Everyone had laughed at the idea of Sally Ingram shoplifting. 'But it must be true,' murmured Frankie, staring at the print. She hugged herself as she realised what power the camera was giving her. It could show her the deepest secrets of anyone she cared to photograph.

She moved on to the third picture, the one of Ian Elliot, and looked at the scrawled lines for a long time. Her face grew serious and her eyes glittered with tears. Suddenly, she ran out of the bathroom and up to the camera.

'He was my friend,' quavered Frankie and her mouth turned down at the corners. 'I liked him. I didn't want to know that. I didn't want to know!'

Frankie began to cry. Suddenly she felt very alone. She grabbed the curtain that was covering the window-seat cushions and flung it over the camera, then she screwed up the print and threw it down on the floor. Finally, she curled up on her bed and turned her back on the tented shape that crouched in the middle of her room.

6

When the classroom door opened, Alice twisted round in her seat to look, but it was only little Steven Grant with a message from the school office.

'Alice,' boomed Mr Chester. 'Will you please stop your Monday morning bottom-shuffling and get on with your work? What is so fascinating about that door today?'

'Nothing, sir. Sorry, sir,' said Alice, with a sideways glance at Frankie's empty desk.

'Oh, I see,' said Mr Chester, following her glance. 'You're wondering where your friend Frankie is.' He ripped open the envelope from the office and unfolded the message inside. 'Aha. Well I can tell you that Frankie won't be in today, so you can settle down now.'

In the desk opposite Alice, David did not look up from his book, but the tension went out of his shoulders and he relaxed back into his seat. He had not been looking forward to being in the same room as Frankie Madigan after what had happened the day before.

'Is she – all right, sir?' asked Alice.

'Oh, yes. But she is officially off school this week.

Her father has filled in a holiday form.' Mr Chester waved the form in the air with an expression of distaste before he clipped it into the register. 'As if you lot don't get enough holidays as it is.'

Alice looked down at her bag with the book of Borderlands legends poking out of it. What now? She sat impatiently until the bell rang for break, then she rushed outside to meet Michael.

It was a freezing morning. The school perched up on the cliffs outside the old town walls, and it caught the full blast of the wind blowing off the North Sea. There was snow in the wind as Alice hurried across the yard, and a bank of low grey cloud was moving in overhead.

'Where is she?' asked Michael as Alice jogged around the corner of the gym and huddled into the doorway beside him.

'Her dad's arranged for her to spend some time with her mum. She's off all week. On holiday.' Alice shivered as she peered through the snow flurries to the deserted Holiday Centre below the school and the steel-grey sea beyond. 'Not exactly holiday weather, is it? She hates the cold.' Alice felt sad, suddenly, thinking about Frankie. 'I miss her,' she said.

'But what are we going to do if we can't talk to her at school?' asked Michael. 'How are we going to persuade her to read the book? We won't be able to see her at home, that's for sure. Not after yesterday. She won't let us in.'

'I don't know,' sighed Alice. 'We need David. He's good at ideas.'

Michael jumped up and down on the spot and banged his hands together for warmth. 'No chance of him helping. You saw what he was like this morning. He won't even talk about her. He's so stubborn, sometimes!'

'Leave him to me,' said Alice. 'I'll talk him round. Wait for us at the end of school.'

'This had better be good,' growled David, as he stood with Alice and Michael at the gates and watched his school bus disappearing down the street. 'My mum's doing stew and dumplings tonight.'

'You know you can eat with us,' said Alice. 'And my dad'll run you home afterwards. But first, we need to talk. Come on. Let's walk around the town walls.'

'You're not serious, are you?' asked David, looking at the darkening sky and the dusting of dry snow blowing across the pavement. But Alice was already plodding away down the street.

David raised his eyebrows at Michael. 'She's been drinking anti-freeze again, hasn't she?' he said. Michael giggled but then turned along the street after Alice and David had to follow.

Alice had chosen the walls on purpose. Usually, she was afraid of heights, but she didn't mind the fortified walls. They were as wide and flat as two streets put together, and they circled the town like an elevated race track. She had chosen the walls because, once David was up there, he would find it hard to leave them and stalk off when the talk turned to Frankie. There was only one path to follow.

The walls were quiet. The cold weather had kept most people indoors. Alice put her head down against the wind and walked on in silence, with Michael beside her, waiting for David's curiosity to get the better of him.

'All right then,' pleaded David finally. 'Tell me what the big mystery is, before I freeze to death.'

Alice stopped and moved over to one of the benches which edged the path. David and Michael sat down on either side of her.

'Where do we start?' asked Michael.

'With this,' said Alice, pulling the book from her jacket pocket. 'David, this is the book you found in Frankie's camera case yesterday.'

'Hey!' protested David, springing to his feet. 'You said this wasn't about – her.'

'Sit down,' sighed Alice. 'Frankie's only part of this. And when you've heard what we've got to say, you might understand a bit more about why she's behaving like she is.'

David hesitated, then shoved his hands into his pockets and came back to the bench.

'OK. Me and Michael, we think Mrs Fraser –'

'– the housekeeper –'

'– at the auction. We think she was –' Alice took a deep breath, '– telling the truth about the camera. Don't! Don't say anything, David. Just listen for a minute. Think how Frankie's been acting over that camera, the way she won't let anyone touch it. It's not like her at all. You said yourself, she always shares everything.'

David nodded, reluctantly.

'Mrs Fraser said the camera would make her like that, remember? And she called it a web weaver. Webs are to trap things in, aren't they?'

'Like that camera's trapped Frankie,' said Michael. He shuddered. 'It's got her almost – hypnotised.'

'So, what's the book got to do with it?' asked David.

'All right, we know that the man who owned that house at the end of the last century was an explorer and a collector. And we know that he liked to collect – strange things.'

David nodded again, remembering some of the oddities he had seen in the auction. Alice continued, encouraged by the nod.

'And the camera was one of the strange things he collected. He knew it could – could –' Alice looked at Michael, wondering how to explain the hold the camera had over Frankie. It had all seemed much clearer the night before, when she and Michael had talked late into the evening.

'It's like Mrs Fraser said,' Michael began. 'That camera can make a person want to use it. We're not sure, but we think Frankie is expecting the camera to take – special – photographs. Photographs that show more than a normal camera would.'

'That's stupid –' David started, but Alice interrupted him.

'There's a label stuck on the underside of the camera, David. We think the man who found the camera on his travels put the label there. He wrote three words on the label. A sort of question.'

'Yes?' prompted David.

'It says, "*Seeing is believing?*"'

'It's a warning, do you see?' said Michael, eagerly. 'He's telling people not to believe what the camera shows them. And this book –'

'He put a clue in here too,' said Alice, opening the book to show David the label.

David leaned forward to look at the faded handwriting. '"*The greater truth?*"' he read. He looked up at Alice and Michael and his face was full of confusion. 'I don't get it.'

'We think this book is like the antidote to the camera. We think Mrs Fraser might have put it in the box on purpose, when she realised the camera had got a hold on Frankie.'

David took the book. '*Tales from the Truth Teller?*'

Alice opened her mouth but Michael laid a warning hand on her arm. She turned to look at him and he put a finger to his lips. Alice saw that David was no longer perching on the edge of the bench. He was sitting down properly, looking through the book. She nodded to Michael to show that she understood, then she sat back and waited.

'They're stories,' said David. 'How can they help?'

Wordlessly, Alice turned to the line drawing and pointed to the writing underneath.

'"*I promise you one thing, reader,*"' read David. '"*My tales will never deceive you, for I am the Truth Teller. My life is in these tales. Call them stories if*

62

you must, but remember, sometimes stories carry a greater truth within."'

He looked up and smiled. 'I like that. What are they about?'

'He was a traveller, then a shepherd,' said Alice. 'His real name was Thomas Laidlaw, but by the end of his life, everyone knew him as the Truth Teller because he would never tell a lie. The stories start when he was a young man and he was kidnapped by the Good People and –'

'Good People?' asked David.

'Faeries,' said Alice.

'That's it!' said David in disgust, leaping to his feet. 'I'm not listening to any more of this rubbish!'

'No!' Alice jumped up and grabbed at his arm. 'They're like fables, these stories. You have to look for the truth in them. The Good People, they were supposed to make people see things that weren't really there. He says they had the power of – of glamour. They could make worthless stones look like pieces of gold – stuff like that. All he's really saying is that when he was younger, he was taken in by appearances. By lies.'

David sat down slowly. 'You mean like Frankie being taken in by the camera?'

'Yes. And as he grew older he began to see through all that. He travelled all over the place, but he ended up choosing to live on Cheildon Hill as a shepherd. He says there's no deceit, no glamour, up on the side of Cheildon, just the bare truth.'

David frowned. 'So, you think if you can get

63

Frankie to read this book, she might start to see sense about the camera?'

Alice nodded. 'We need your help, David.'

'No way,' said David.

'Please? She'll listen to you.'

'She hit me. She called me a liar.'

'Come on, David,' cried Alice. 'What have we just been trying to tell you? That wasn't Frankie! Not the real Frankie! The web weaver's got her.'

David stood up and looked down at them. 'You can't blame the camera for Frankie telling us her mum was dead. She didn't have the camera then,' he said quietly. 'She told that lie all on her own.'

Alice stared at David for a few seconds, then raised her hands in defeat. 'You're right,' she said simply. 'Frankie lied to us. But she's still our friend and she needs our help. Please, David?'

'No.' David shook his head. 'I never want to talk to her again.'

'You might not have a choice,' said Michael, pointing over David's shoulder.

They turned to look. There were three people battling along the broad back of the wall. Leading the way, side by side, were Mr and Mrs Madigan. Bringing up the rear, stomping along with her head down, was Frankie.

'I'm leaving,' said David.

'You can't!' hissed Alice as Mr Madigan saw them and waved. 'What would Frankie's dad think?'

So David stood, stony-faced, between Alice and Michael as the Madigan family approached.

'Hi, you three!' called Mr Madigan. Frankie's head jerked up and she gave them a startled glance before turning her face away.

'So, we aren't the only mad people out here today, then?' smiled Mrs Madigan, peeking out at them from between the folds of at least three scarves.

'It's not like California weather, is it?' said Alice, glancing nervously between David and Frankie.

'You can say that again. I hope the snow clears up by Friday. I'm taking Frances to Edinburgh, to see if I can find her some decent clothes.'

Alice kept her eyes firmly on Mrs Madigan but she was still aware of Frankie raising her head and glaring at her mother.

'Um, so how long are you staying?' asked Alice.

'Just for the week. I fly back on Sunday.'

'We'll miss her, won't we, honey?' said Mr Madigan. Frankie put her head down and did not answer.

'Uh, we decided Frankie here needed some air,' continued Mr Madigan. 'She's been fussing with that snakey camera all day, taking photographs of all our visitors in the morning and developing the prints this afternoon. Not that it seems to have made her very happy . . .' He looked round at his daughter and frowned anxiously.

'Hey!' he said, turning back to them. 'I have an idea. Why don't you come home with us for a while? We have cookies. We have hot chocolate. We have warm radiators.'

'Well . . .' said Alice. She looked at David, waiting for him to decide.

'You can phone your parents from there. What do you say? I think Frankie would like that. Wouldn't you, honey?' Mr Madigan stepped from in front of Frankie and they got their first good look at her. Her eyes were very big and dark, as though she had not slept at all. She was trying to look bored, but a mixture of expressions was fighting to come through. Loneliness, pleasure at seeing them, and – most of all – fear. Frankie looked very, very frightened.

David stared hard at Frankie. She looked so bad, he wanted to put his arms around her, but he still felt betrayed. How could he stay friends with her when their whole friendship was built on a lie? He knew he would never have put up with her in those early days if she hadn't told him about her mum being dead. But then, maybe that would have been his loss? Maybe Alice was right. Frankie was their friend and they should help her, whatever she had done.

David stared at Frankie and struggled to decide. 'Cookies?' he said finally. 'I'll go for that.'

7

'Great!' said Mr Madigan. 'Cookies it is. And the chocolatiest hot chocolate you've ever tasted, with plenty of whipped cream. Shall we head for home, before my feet fall off?'

'You two go on,' said Frankie. 'We'll meet you at the house. I'd like to, um, take a longer walk first.'

'You? Walk further?' said Mr Madigan.

'You? Stay out in the cold?' said Mrs Madigan.

Frankie's parents stared at her with identical expressions of surprise and Alice started to snort with laughter. She couldn't help it. She always turned giggly in tense situations and their faces looked so comical, it started her off.

Mr and Mrs Madigan turned to look at Alice with the same surprised expressions, which made her snort even more loudly.

'I – I'm so-orry,' she gasped. 'It's just . . . your faces . . .'

Michael had started sniggering beside her and suddenly Alice was laughing so hard, she couldn't finish her sentence.

'You'll have to excuse these two,' said David, glaring at Alice and Michael as they leaned together with tears streaming down their faces. 'They always set each other off like this.'

David tried to keep frowning, but his mouth turned itself up at the corners and then he was laughing too, hooting great clouds of white vapour into the freezing air.

Frankie was the last to crumble. She held out until Michael fell over and began beating at the ground with his gloved hand, gasping for breath and groaning as though he was in pain. As Frankie watched him, a single yelp escaped from her mouth. She looked surprised for an instant, then her whole body seemed to relax. She fell back on to the bench, threw out her arms and laughed until her sides ached.

Mr Madigan watched Frankie laugh with a look of huge relief. 'Shall we go?' he said to his wife.

'What, and just leave them here, rolling about?'

'Uh-huh. Best thing we could do, I think.'

They laughed themselves to a standstill. One by one, Michael, Alice and David picked themselves up off the cold ground and flopped down on the bench alongside Frankie. For a while they just sat together quietly, apart from the odd tired chuckle. Frankie wiped her face on her sleeve and gazed out at the sea. Everything looked sharp and clear. She smiled, feeling as though she had broken free of a bleak fog which had been wrapped around her for days.

The wind had dropped and it was very still and quiet. There was a pause, then it finally began to snow properly. Great big feathery flakes of white were suddenly all around them, dropping soundlessly from the heavy grey clouds. The snow settled on Frankie's dark hair and on her face as she stared up into the sky.

'I'm sorry, guys,' she said.

Alice reached out and patted her on the arm. Frankie cleared her throat and carried on. 'I'm sorry I told you my mom was – you know. I was scared. See, whenever Dad went off somewhere before, with his work, she would go, too. We all went together.' Frankie shrugged. 'This time, she wouldn't. They fought about it. They fought about it a lot. They got tired of arguing and they didn't say much at all for a while. Then we came out here – and she stayed there.'

Alice nodded, understanding. 'So you thought –'

'They say it's only a work thing. She doesn't want to give up her job but he has to go where the work is. They say we'll be back together at the end of a year. But I'm still scared. What if Mom's found someone else to love? What if they split up?'

'They seem OK together,' said Michael.

'They argue, sometimes.'

'But everyone does that,' said Alice.

'Yeah,' Frankie sighed. 'But every time they do it, I think – you know.'

'Have you told them you're scared?'

Frankie shook her head. 'What if it's true? What if I say, "Hey, guys, I've got this idea in my head that you two might split up. Isn't it silly?" What if I say that and they don't laugh? What if they look all

serious and say, "Well, now you come to mention it
. . ." No, I'd rather not say anything.'

Alice nodded and glanced across at David. He
still had not spoken. Frankie was looking at him
too, out of the corner of her eye. 'Come on,' said
Alice, jumping to her feet. 'Let's walk. I'm getting cold.'

The four of them trudged along the walls through
the falling snow, watching the red rooftops of the
town turn white below them. Frankie edged across
until she was next to David and for a while they
walked side by side in silence, listening to their boots
crunch the snow underfoot.

'Davey? You didn't mess up the prints. I know that
now. I'm sorry.'

'You called me a liar.'

'I know. That was dreadful. I'm sorry.'

They walked on. David pulled a sweet from his
pocket and offered it to Frankie. She took it, held it
in her hand and smiled.

'So what was it?' said David, finally.

'What?'

'You said you knew it wasn't me who messed up
the prints. What was it?'

'Oh.' Frankie stopped on the path and they clustered around her, waiting. 'Look, guys. I know you're
going to think I'm lying again, but I've got to tell you.
I – I think that crazy housekeeper was right.'

Frankie cringed, waiting for them to shout her
down, but they only nodded. She blinked and carried
on. 'I think the camera is kind of strange. It can . . .'

Frankie hesitated then pulled a print from the pocket of her coat. 'Look.'

The print was crumpled, as though it had been screwed up. Frankie lifted her knee and smoothed the print over it as best she could, then she handed the print to David.

'I've already seen this,' he said. 'It's the one we took of Mr Elliot.'

'Yeah, but don't look at the print. Look at the scribbles.'

David, Alice and Michael stared at the scrawling mess.

'Can't you see it?' asked Frankie. 'It's like a cartoon. See, he's got these big fists drawn on the end of his arms and he's got one fist around this woman's neck –'

'That's supposed to be a woman?'

'Yes, I see it,' said Michael, taking the print. 'He's holding her round the neck and she's got a black eye and he's – he's punching her with the other fist.'

Frankie let out a sob and they all turned to look at her. 'He was my friend!' she said.

Alice shook her head. 'Frankie, I don't get it.'

'The camera put these scribbles on the film.'

'How?'

Frankie shrugged. 'I can't work out how, but I know it's the camera. I sit people down in front of it and it looks at them and it can see . . . It can see their secrets. It sees their secrets and it shows them to me. But it only ever shows me horrible secrets. Things I don't want to know.'

'Ian Elliot wouldn't hit a woman!' said David incredulously.

'I thought that too,' said Frankie. 'But . . . Do you remember that time I went out on the survey boat with Dad and Ian?'

'Yes.'

'Well, Dad got into an argument with one of the crew. I heard it. This man told Dad that Ian had been married once, but his wife left him.'

'That's no secret. Everybody knows that –'

'But this man said Ian's wife left him because he beat her up. Dad told the man to shut up and stop spreading lies. But now,' Frankie held out the print and her hand was shaking, 'it seems that man was telling the truth.'

Alice and Michael stared at the print in horror, but David planted his feet solidly on the path and folded his arms. 'That is rubbish.' He took the print out of Michael's hand and screwed it up into a little ball. 'Can't you recognise a lie when you see it?'

'No. It's the truth,' said Frankie. 'They all are.' Her mouth trembled.

'Come on,' said David, turning up his collar against the thickening snow. 'Let's go to your place. We've got something to show you.'

'They're not lies,' repeated Frankie, shaking her head.

David leaned forward over the kitchen table and stared into Frankie's face. 'Yes. They are,' he said.

'Wait till you see the rest of the prints. You'll know.'

David looked helplessly at Alice and Michael.

'All right,' said Michael. 'Let's say those prints really are showing you true secrets. You still shouldn't trust that camera. Somehow, in some way, you're being tricked, Frankie. It's a web weaver!'

'Cameras don't lie,' said Frankie stubbornly. 'They only show what's there.'

Alice leaned back in her chair and wiped the chocolate froth from her mouth. 'Will you at least read the book?'

Frankie shrugged, but she did not put the little book down. She hung on to it as though it was a life-line.

'Will you?'

Frankie nodded, then pushed her chair away from the kitchen table. 'Come on. I'll show you the other prints. Then you'll see what I mean.'

The four of them climbed the stairs to Frankie's room in silence. Alice, Michael and David were all frightened. It had been hard to accept that the camera was dangerous. It was even harder, now, to face it again. For Frankie, something much worse was happening. The fog was coming back. By the time she reached her bedroom, it was as though the walk on the walls had never happened. She moved slowly into the room and drifted over to the camera.

The others stood by the door, not daring to move in too far. Alice scanned the room. The light seemed dull and dingy. The bed was unmade. The presents were still stacked in the corner, unopened. Alice made herself look at the camera. The web weaver. It crouched in the middle of the floor, sleek and shiny. The brass gleamed. The wood glowed. Somehow, it had become the most attractive thing in the room. Alice had a strong urge to pick the camera up and throw it through the window.

Frankie seemed to sense this and she moved to stand between them and the camera.

'So,' said David. 'Where are they?'

'What?' said Frankie.

'The rest of the prints.'

'Oh, them. No, you can't see them.'

'But that's what we came up here for.'

'Yeah, but, I tore them all up.'

David scowled. 'Even the ones you did today?'

'Yeah. I forgot. Sorry.'

Michael sighed. 'We've lost her again,' he said quietly.

'It's tricking you, Frankie,' said David. 'Cameras can lie. You know that.'

Frankie slammed the Truth Teller's book down on top of her bookcase and picked up a box file instead. She upended the file and photographs of David, Alice and Michael spilled out and fanned across the carpet.

Alice gasped. She knew that Frankie thought nothing of using up a whole film in a few minutes, but still she was surprised by the number of photographs spread out in front of her. 'You took all these?' she asked.

74

Frankie was scrabbling through the pile, selecting prints. 'Here,' she said, laying out the shots she had chosen. 'Look at these. I've been taking them over the last couple of months.'

They stared at the prints and a silence grew in the room. There was Michael, hunched and anxious, scurrying out of his flat and sending a frightened look back at his father. David had been caught as he spoke at a photography club meeting. He looked smug and self-satisfied and totally unaware of the bored expressions on the faces around him. Alice was standing at a shop window gazing in at the display. A carnival of bright, lively clothes glowed in the window and Alice stood in front of them in her limp, over-washed top and her outgrown trousers, like a long, thin smudge on the glass.

'See?' Frankie demanded, and Alice could not help but nod. Frankie's photographs did not lie. They were cruel, very cruel, but they were true. Alice smoothed down her school skirt, suddenly very aware of how creased it was. Michael stared at his pinched face in the photograph and his hands began to twist together.

'I've had enough of this,' said David. 'Where are those prints? In there?' He started to walk towards the bathroom but Frankie darted across the floor before he had taken more than two steps. Quickly, she took the key from the inside of the door and locked the bathroom from the outside.

'There's nothing in there,' said Frankie, slipping the key into her pocket.

'Yes there is,' said David. 'All my developing stuff's in there. And I want it back.'

Frankie's eyes grew wide with shock. 'You can't do that! I need it.'

'And I want it back. I don't like what you're using it for.'

Frankie's face grew hard. She stalked over to her bedside table and grabbed a fistful of the birthday money her mother had given her. 'Here,' she hissed, flinging the notes on to the pile of photographs. 'Buy yourself some more. And close the door on your way out.'

'You know what you should do?' said David. 'If you really want to know about your mum and dad, you should put them in front of your precious web weaver and see what it tells you.'

'David!' protested Alice.

'But cameras never lie,' said David, mimicking Frankie. 'Do they?' He kicked the money and photographs out of his path and strode from the room.

'You really shouldn't do what he said –' began Alice.

'Go!' interrupted Frankie. 'Both of you.'

Frankie stood, still and tense, until the front door slammed shut, then she turned to stare at the camera. Her face was troubled. Quickly, she picked up the velvet curtain from the floor and threw it over the camera. Then she collected the little book from the shelf where she had left it. Frankie sat on her bed, wrapped the duvet around her, and began to read.

*   *   *

'What are we going to do now?' asked Michael as they left Frankie's house.

'Leave her to it,' said David, his voice still tight with anger.

Michael sighed. 'You shouldn't have said that, about her parents and the camera.' He paused, but David remained stubbornly silent. 'Well, at least she kept the book. It might be all right, if she reads the book.'

They trudged down the street in silence, through the deepening snow. 'I know what we have to do,' said Alice. 'We have to destroy that camera.'

'Oh, OK, then,' said David sarcastically. 'I'll just go and get a sledge hammer.'

'I'm serious,' said Alice.

'Frankie won't let us near it,' said Michael.

'But she won't be in on Friday. You heard Mrs Madigan. She's taking Frankie to Edinburgh.'

David scooped up a handful of snow and moulded it into a ball. He threw the snowball at a post box and missed. 'I see. We're going to break in, are we?' He scooped up another handful of snow.

'No. We knock on the door and ask Mr Madigan if we can nip up and get something we left in Frankie's room.'

David was about to throw a second snowball, but he stopped and lowered his arm. 'Yes. That would work. But we can't just smash up the camera, can we? Do you know how much that thing cost? What would Mr Madigan say?'

Michael stopped and turned to stare back at the

house. He was remembering Mr Madigan's anxious face as he looked at Frankie. 'Do you know,' he said thoughtfully, 'I don't think her dad would mind very much. He knows something's wrong.'

Alice took the snowball from David's hand and splatted it accurately against the side of the post box. 'We have to do it,' she said, simply. 'If we want Frankie back.'

8

Over the next four days, the snow fell and settled, thawed and fell again. By the time they stood in a huddle at the corner of Frankie's street after school on Friday, there was a patchy mix of puddles, slush and ice underfoot.

'Mr Madigan's in. The car's there,' said Alice.

'Thanks for pointing that out,' said David, irritably. 'I'd never have worked that out for myself.'

He shoved his hands deep into his pockets and stamped his feet. His shoes were letting in water and his feet were wet and cold, but that was not the reason for his irritation. He was unsure about what they were planning to do and David hated to be unsure.

Alice gave David a look, then carried on. 'All right, are we ready?'

Michael and David both held up their empty sports bags. They were planning to split the camera from the tripod, then use the bags to smuggle it past Mr Madigan and out of the house.

'We'll take it to my place,' said Alice. 'Then we can decide how to get rid of it.'

Michael shifted uncomfortably. 'The web weaver.

It's not dangerous to take it, is it? It can't – hurt us?'

'I don't think so. But you never know . . .' Alice shuddered. 'We shouldn't hang about once we've got it. I'm for burning it.'

'But if there is acid inside, it might explode or something. We could throw it off the cliffs.'

'No.' Alice shook her head. 'We couldn't be sure, that way.'

'I'm not sure we should even be taking it,' said David.

'What if they haven't gone to Edinburgh?' asked Michael. 'They might have stayed home in this weather.'

'Frankie's bedroom lights are off, stupid,' sighed David. 'She's not going to be sitting up there in the dark, is she . . . ?'

David trailed off. They all stared up at Frankie's bedroom windows, imagining her and the camera standing silently together in the shadows, waiting for them.

'This is getting silly,' said Alice firmly. 'Of course she's not up there. And there's only one way to find out whether they went to Edinburgh. Come on.' She set off for Frankie's house.

Alice rang the bell and waited. A shadowy figure appeared behind the frosted glass of the door. 'We're all right so far,' she whispered. 'It's him.'

'Well, hi!' said Mr Madigan when he opened the door. He sounded genuinely pleased to see them. David felt like crawling away.

'Hello, Mr Madigan,' said Alice, brightly. 'Is Frankie in?'

'Gee, I'm sorry. She's out shopping with her mom.'

'Oh, that's a shame,' said Alice loudly, to cover Michael's sigh of relief. 'I wanted to see her because she's got my maths book and I need it for the weekend.'

'Well, why don't you go up and look for it?' said Mr Madigan, swinging the door open to let them in. 'She won't mind. I'm cooking right now, so I'll leave you to it, OK?'

Mr Madigan disappeared into the kitchen and left them in the hallway.

'That was easy,' whispered Michael.

'Let's hope the rest is,' said Alice, heading for the stairs.

'Wait!' David shuffled his feet and looked towards the kitchen. 'I'm not sure about this. It doesn't seem right –'

'Do you want Frankie back? I do!' said Alice. Tears filled her eyes and she turned away to hide them. She stomped off up the stairs and, without another word, they followed.

Frankie's bedroom door was slightly open. Alice peered through the gap. A thin wedge of light stretched across the floor from the landing, touching on the unopened presents and resting on the bed. Alice stared at the bed and smiled. The book lay on the pillow, as though Frankie had been reading it.

The sight gave Alice the courage to slide her hand into the dark room and find the light switch.

She flicked the light on and turned to David and Michael.

'Ready?' she asked. They nodded and she put her hand flat against the door and pushed. Slowly, the door swung open. They stood in the doorway, waiting for the camera to come into view, but there was no dark shape crouched in the middle of Frankie's room. The web weaver had gone.

'Oh no!' cried Alice, running to the place where the camera had stood. She turned on the spot, scanning the corners of the room. 'Where is it?'

'I know,' said David. He walked over to the bathroom door and tried the handle. 'Locked,' he said. 'She's locked it in there.'

'Do you think she guessed what we were going to do?' asked Alice.

'Either that, or she just doesn't trust anyone any more.'

Alice and David looked at one another, hopelessly. 'What now?' asked David.

'I really don't know,' said Alice, and her voice trembled. 'That was my best idea.'

They trudged back downstairs in silence.

'Did you find what you wanted?' asked Mr Madigan, popping his head out of the kitchen.

'No,' sighed Alice, without thinking. 'I – I mean –'

'That's too bad. I know! Why don't you call round tomorrow morning? We'll be in. Frankie's decided she wants to shoot us with her snakey camera.'

'What? Who?' gasped Alice.

'Me and her mom,' said Mr Madigan.

'Together?'

'Yeah.' Mr Madigan leaned towards them. 'To be honest,' he said. 'I don't like the thing. It's creepy, that noise it makes. But, hey, it seems like it's a big thing to Frankie, so what the heck. That's what we'll be doing tomorrow morning, if you want to drop by.'

Alice opened her mouth to accept the invitation but Michael spoke first. 'No thanks, Mr Madigan,' he said. 'We've got to be somewhere else.'

'So where have we got to be all of a sudden?' hissed Alice, as the front door closed behind them. 'Didn't you hear him? Frankie's decided to use the web weaver on them tomorrow.'

'I know. We can't stop her.'

'We could have at least tried! There's nothing else left to do.'

'Yes there is,' said Michael quietly. 'I think it's time we went back to the house. I think it's time we talked to Mrs Fraser.'

'Another freeze last night, then,' said the woman, leaning against the handrail at the front of the bus.

'You don't need to tell me that,' said the driver grimly, as he eased around a bend in the icy road.

Alice nudged David in the ribs as the big house came into view around the corner. Michael jumped up and pushed the bell.

'More snow to come, too,' said the woman, staring up at the low grey sky. 'That'll drop before tonight.'

'Thanks,' muttered the driver as he pulled to a stop at the bottom of the driveway. 'That's really cheered me up.'

Alice, David and Michael climbed down from the bus and stood together on the verge.

'Could have told you we wouldn't get a proper thaw,' said the woman to the driver as the bus doors hissed shut. 'Look at Cheildon. All over white.'

The dirt-streaked side of the bus moved away and there in front of them, rising out of the snowy fields like a huge scoop of ice-cream, stood the massive bulk of Cheildon Hill.

'Pity,' said David, staring at the hill.

'What's a pity?'

'That she didn't read the book.'

'I don't know,' said Alice. 'I think she did read it. It was on her pillow yesterday.'

'Didn't do much good, then, did it?'

Alice shrugged and gazed up at Cheildon Hill. The snow had smoothed it out, rounding off the crags and filling in all the hollows. She thought of Thomas Laidlaw searching those same hollows for lost sheep hundreds of years ago.

'You never know,' she said.

'Frances, why aren't you wearing that great dress I bought you yesterday?'

Frankie lifted her head for a second and gave her mother a dark-eyed stare before she ducked back behind the camera.

'Leave her be,' said Mr Madigan out of the corner

of his mouth as he sat by his wife in the window seat.

'But grey is such a great colour for you, Frances. And so – understated,' she added, frowning at Frankie's orange shorts and tiger-stripe tights.

Frankie straightened up from the camera. 'OK. The focus is just right. Don't move now.'

'She likes bright colours,' hissed Mr Madigan, as Frankie bent to take a new film case from the mahogany box. 'And do you have to keep calling her Frances? She hates it.'

Frankie slotted the case into the side of the camera and hesitated, staring at her parents.

'Do we have to go into that again?' said Mrs Madigan, patting her hair into place for the photograph. 'I called her Frances, not Frankie.'

'Guys . . .' said Frankie, stepping away from the camera.

'But she wants to be called Frankie. The poor kid's been asking you for years. Why won't you give in?'

'Guys?'

'Oh, yeah, and have both her parents spoiling her silly?'

Frankie sighed and walked back to the camera. She grasped the edge of the film casing and her parents turned away from one another to face the lens. Frankie pulled back the case to expose the film.

'Smile,' she said.

'Ready?' asked Michael. Alice and David stared at the

glossy green door of the lodge house. Alice swallowed nervously and nodded her head.

'Go on,' said David.

Michael pressed the doorbell. Inside, something skittered to the door and began to hiss and snuffle along the bottom edge. They took a step back.

'What's that?' whispered David, nervously.

Footsteps approached the door. There was a scuffling sound and the hissing stopped. Then the lock turned and the door opened. A smiling woman stood in the doorway, holding a Border Terrier puppy in her arms. She was wearing yellow rubber gloves and the puppy was chewing the end of one of the fingers. The fresh scent of pine cleaner drifted from the house behind her.

They all stared. This was not the gaunt, frightening woman they remembered from the day of the auction. This woman was pink in the face and smiling and really quite pretty.

'Can I help you?' said the woman.

'Mrs Fraser?' asked Michael, doubtfully. The woman peered more closely at the children and, suddenly, her smile disappeared.

'It is Mrs Fraser,' said Michael more confidently, as her dark eyes fixed on him. 'You said to come back, if we needed to.'

'The web weaver?' said Mrs Fraser and Michael nodded.

The housekeeper sighed. 'I thought – when you didn't come . . . I thought it must be all right.'

Michael shook his head and Mrs Fraser stepped

back to let them in. 'You'll have to take me as you find me,' she said. 'I'm in the middle of cleaning up. You can leave your boots on that newspaper there.'

Mrs Fraser closed the front door and put the puppy down. She walked down the tiny hallway and through a door on the left. As they bent to untie laces, they could hear water running into a kettle and the clink of cups. The puppy was busy sniffing at their boots, his tail wagging furiously. It all seemed so – normal.

When they padded into the kitchen in their socks, Mrs Fraser was sitting at the table with a pot of tea and a plate of biscuits waiting for them.

'Tell me,' she said, filling their cups.

'It's just as you said it would be,' Alice began. 'The camera's got Frankie. She's – obsessed with it. She can't leave it alone, even though it's making her very unhappy.'

Mrs Fraser frowned. 'Are you telling me the camera still has a hold on her?'

Alice nodded.

'But didn't you find the Truth Teller's book, in the camera box?' asked Mrs Fraser.

'Yes, we gave it to her.'

'And has she read it?'

'I think so,' said Alice.

'Then she really is in trouble,' sighed Mrs Fraser. 'You see, the web weaver binds its victim more and more tightly with each photograph it takes. The only way to break the hold of the web weaver is to destroy the camera, but this must be done in a certain way.'

'How?' asked David.

'The answer lies in the book,' said Mrs Fraser. 'If Frankie is still trapped by the web weaver, then she must have read the book too late. She is too deep in the trap to see the way out. Has she used the camera a lot?'

'I'm not sure,' said Alice. 'I don't think she's taken that many photographs.'

'In that case . . .' Mrs Fraser hesitated.

'Yes?' asked David.

'Some people fall into the trap of the web weaver more easily than others. If a person does not have a strong feel for the truth. If a person tends to . . .'

'Lie?' asked David.

Mrs Fraser nodded.

'That's Frankie,' said David bleakly.

Mrs Fraser leaned across the table and stared at Alice. 'Tell me about the photographs.'

'They come out with all these white scribbles over the top of the print.'

'It's not the developing,' said David. 'I did some of them myself and I know I did it right.'

Mrs Fraser waved her hand impatiently. 'Of course it's not the developing. It's the camera. And the scribbles? What about them?'

They looked at one another, each reluctant to say what the scribbles showed. 'They seem to be deliberate,' said Michael, finally. 'They seem to be – drawings.'

'Of?'

'Of secrets. The secrets of the people in the photographs.'

'Aha.'

'Mrs Fraser, Frankie believes the camera is telling her the truth, but we know it must be tricking her. The trouble is, we don't know exactly how.'

'I'll tell you what I know,' said Mrs Fraser, settling back in her chair. 'Mr Weston, the man I worked for until he died, he told me his great grandfather found the web weaver in London, way back in nineteen hundred.'

'His great grandfather was the traveller?'

'That's right. He was staying near the docks in London, waiting for a ship. A local man, a very jealous husband, had killed his wife and his brother with an axe and, when he was arrested, he was trying to smash up the camera with the same axe he'd used to kill them.'

'You mean those cuts in the side of the camera were done by a murderer?' Alice asked.

'So the story goes.'

'With the murder weapon?' Alice felt the back of her neck turn cold. She had rubbed her fingers over those gashes in the wood.

'All the neighbours knew was that the man had taken a photograph of his brother and his wife together, the day before the brother was due to emigrate to America. The next morning they were dead. Murdered. Mr Weston's great grandfather was there when they carted the man off to prison,' continued Mrs Fraser. 'The man kept shouting that the camera had tricked him. He called it a web weaver and said it was evil.

'Well, no one in the street wanted to touch the thing after that, so Mr Weston's great grandfather took it back to his lodgings and had a good look at it. It seemed to be an ordinary camera to him, but there was a man in prison, blaming it for the death of two people. He was curious. He went to see the man in prison, the night before he was hanged. The man was quite mad by then. You see, he had got it into his head that his brother was planning to run off to America with his wife, but after he had killed them, he could only find one lot of travel tickets in his brother's chest. All the man kept saying was, "The web weaver makes your worst fear come true."'

Frankie's hands were shaking as she lifted the print from the tray. She had known back at the processing stage what the photograph would show – it was obvious even on the negative – but she had gone on working her way mechanically through every stage in the developing process. She had been hoping the image would change.

Frankie clipped the print to the drying line and turned on the main light. She raised her eyes to the print as it hung exposed under the bright light and she began to cry. Tears slid down her cheeks and dripped from her chin as she stared at the photograph. There was only one mark on the print. It was a line. A jagged white line. It cut through the print from top to bottom, splitting her parents apart.

*   *   *

'It makes your worst fear come true? What did he mean?' asked David.

'Mr Weston's great grandfather had an idea what was happening,' said Mrs Fraser. 'He tried to find out where the camera had come from. He traced it back through six owners and two miserable, destructive years before he lost the trail in France. The web weaver was brought back here to the big house and Mr Weston's great grandfather tried an experiment. What he did was, he paid a model to pose for the camera. He told every member of the household a different lie about the model, then he got each one to take a photograph. Now, what do you think the photographs showed?'

David and Alice looked across the table at one another, their faces blank, but Michael was nodding fiercely. 'Of course,' he breathed. 'Each photograph had a different drawing on it, didn't it?'

Mrs Fraser nodded. 'Whatever lie a person had been told, that's what showed up on the photograph they took.'

'You mean, the camera read their minds?'

'In a very limited way,' agreed Mrs Fraser. 'The web weaver can somehow pick up the photographer's worst fears about the person in the lens. It can pick up those fears, however deep they are buried, and put them on to the film.'

'So it doesn't show the truth?' asked David.

'Ah, now that is why the web weaver is so dangerous,' said Mrs Fraser. 'Sometimes it does show the truth, if the photographer's fears are justified, but not always. The problem is, the victims of the web weaver believe it tells the truth every time.'

Alice jumped up from her chair. 'We've got to get back to Frankie!' she cried. 'She's taking a photograph of her parents to find out whether they're splitting up and –'

'– it'll put her worst fear on the film,' interrupted Michael.

'She'll think it's the truth,' said David. 'Mrs Fraser, when's the next bus back to the coast?'

'In about two minutes,' said the housekeeper, glancing at her watch.

'Quick! We've got to catch it!' cried Alice.

The three of them ran to their boots and pulled them on. They opened the front door and raced out on to the road just as the bus came around the corner.

David was about to follow Alice and Michael up the steps of the bus when he remembered something. He jumped down on to the snowy verge and ran around to the front of the bus. Mrs Fraser was standing at her front door, pulling her cardigan tight about her against the cold. David cupped his hands around his mouth. 'How do we destroy the camera?' he shouted.

Mrs Fraser nodded and shouted a reply, but David could only hear snatches of it above the noise of the bus engine.

'. . . power back on itself . . .' she called, '. . . escape from the Good People . . . in the book . . .'

David thought about running back to the lodge, but the driver was banging on the windscreen above him, so he raised his hand to Mrs Fraser and clambered aboard.

9

Frankie came out of the bathroom and stared at the web weaver. Her face was stained with tears. She looked from the glossy, shining camera to the battered, faded little book lying on her pillow, then back to the camera.

Was seeing believing? Or did the book hold the greater truth? Frankie stared again at the web weaver and her face twisted in misery. She did not want the photograph to be true, but the camera stood there, gleaming and solid, defying her to doubt it. Frankie turned her back on the camera, opened the book at the last page and began to read.

'*I have made my home on Cheildon Hill, and here I shall remain. There is no glamour to deceive me on the bare side of Cheildon. Lies cannot find a hold here, amongst the wind and snow and old, old rock. Only truth grows on Cheildon.*'

'Only truth grows on Cheildon,' said Frankie, looking up at the camera. She jumped to her feet.

'All right then,' she said, pulling her Doc Martens on over her tiger-stripe tights. 'Let's go find out.'

She grabbed her scarlet jacket from the back of the door and dragged it on. Then she jammed a hat over her springy curls and wrapped a scarf around her neck.

She paused at the bedroom door and stared across the room to the print, still hanging in her bathroom. The jagged white line was clear, even from such a distance. Frankie's mouth trembled. She hurried back to the bathroom and pulled the print from the line. At her desk, she grabbed a pen and scrawled a few words across the front of the photograph, then she stepped out of her bedroom and zipped up her jacket.

She moved silently past the kitchen where her parents were talking, eased open the front door and slipped out into the street. The temperature was dropping as she hurried towards the bus station. The sky was darkening and the clouds above her head were heavy with snow.

'You're too late,' said Mr Madigan, when he opened the door to David's knock.

'Too late?' gasped Alice.

'To see us get the hissing treatment. Isn't that what you're here for, to watch us pose for our mug-shot? Frankie took the photograph earlier this morning. She's up there now, developing it. You can go up if you like. Hey! Remember not to open the bathroom door. Darkroom rules!' yelled Mr Madigan as they rushed past him and up the stairs.

'We won't,' called Alice over her shoulder. Mr Madigan shook his head and hurried back to the warmth of the kitchen.

'Frankie!' called Alice, racing into the bedroom after Michael and David. She came to a halt as she spotted the web weaver lurking in the shadows. It looked bigger, somehow. Alice shuddered and turned on the main light. The camera sat on its spindly legs, sleek and fat. Well-fed, thought Alice. She looked away and saw that the bathroom door was open. 'Frankie?' she called.

'Mr Madigan was right,' said Michael, coming out of the bathroom. 'We are too late. She's gone.'

'Oh, no!' Alice looked at the web weaver out of the corner of her eye. 'Did she develop the print of her parents?'

'Looks like it,' called David, from the bathroom. All this stuff's been used this morning. There's no print here, though, as far as I can see.'

'Where do you think she's gone?' wondered Alice.

'Here's the print,' said Michael, turning from the desk. 'And I know where she's gone.' He held out the print and pointed to the words Frankie had scrawled across the front of it.

'"Gone where the truth grows,"' read David. 'What does that mean?'

'That's what the Truth Teller said, at the end of the book,' said Michael. 'Remember? No lies grow on Cheildon, only the truth.'

'She's gone to Cheildon Hill,' said Alice. 'In this weather?'

They all turned to the window and looked out at the darkening sky. The first fat flakes of snow were drifting past the glass.

'We'll have to tell her mum and dad,' said Alice. 'And quickly. It's really dangerous up on Cheildon at this time of year. People die out there! They're going to have to call out Border Search and Rescue.'

Michael swallowed and looked down at the print. 'But, her parents, they'll never believe us.'

'In that case,' said David, taking the print from Michael and stuffing it into the pocket of his trousers, 'we're going to have to do it ourselves. But first,' he turned to glare at the web weaver, crouching fat and sleek in the middle of the floor. 'First, we have to destroy that.'

'David!' cried Alice. 'Frankie's up on Cheildon! On her own! We'll have to leave the web-weaver for later.'

'No,' said David, picking up the Truth Teller's book from Frankie's pillow and leafing through it. 'This first. You heard what Mrs Fraser said. Frankie's not going to see anything as it really is until she's free of the web weaver. We get rid of this thing for her and at least she'll be up there with a clear head. I reckon we'll double her chances of coming back down alive. Ah, here we are. *"I was trapped by the glamour and lies of the Good People for seven years before I found a way to escape . . ."'*

David bent his head and scanned the pages of the book. A smile came to his face. 'It's all done by mirrors!' he laughed, pushing the book into Alice's hands and disappearing into Frankie's bathroom.

'What does it say?' asked Michael.

'It's that bit about him polishing up the shoulder

clasp of his plaid, remember? *"There were no mirrors in the realm of the Good People and the desire to see my own face grew strong in me. I took the round metal clasp from my cloak and polished it so highly it was like a looking glass. I looked into it and saw myself as I really was. The rich clothes I fancied I wore were but my own poor things, fallen into rags. My face was gaunt and bearded and much older than the youth I thought to see. I turned my looking glass towards the beautiful faery queen and she became an old hag upon the instant. Then all the glamour of the Good People fell away from my eyes and I found myself back at the tree I had dozed beneath all those years ago."'*

'Turn the power back upon itself,' said David, hurrying from the bathroom with the wall mirror clutched in his hands. 'That's what Mrs Fraser shouted to me just before I got on the bus. This mirror will destroy the web weaver for us!'

'How?' asked Alice.

'We show it its true self,' said David, moving up to the web weaver. For a few seconds he hesitated, frightened to touch the camera, but the thought of Frankie out on the side of Cheildon alone made him stretch out his hand and pull the cap from the lens.

'Don't!' shouted Michael. David ignored him and reached into the mahogany box for a fresh film case. Quickly he slotted the case into the side of the camera, then he held the mirror up in front of the lens.

'Here goes,' he said, and pulled back the casing to expose the film.

For three seconds, David stood firm, holding the

mirror up to the lens, then he pushed the casing back into the side of the web weaver. His face was white as he stumbled away from the camera. His hands were shaking so much, he nearly dropped the mirror. 'Let's see what it makes of that,' he muttered, moving with Alice and Michael into the far corner of the room.

The web weaver began to hiss as it got to work on the film. Then it stopped. There was a pause, just an instant, before the hissing started up again, quickly rising in pitch and volume until a high, eerie screaming filled the air.

David slammed the bedroom door shut to stop Mr and Mrs Madigan from hearing and the three of them huddled together, watching as the web weaver began to quiver on its tripod. A sickly green light glowed inside the leather abdomen and smoke curled from the lens.

They covered their ears as the shrieking became unbearable. The green glow grew brighter and brighter until it blazed right through the leather concertina like an X-ray, lighting up the skeletal frame inside.

Alice shrank back against David as the quivering became stronger. The camera began to judder so violently that the tripod legs lifted from the floor. Slowly, jerkily, the web weaver turned on the spot until the bright green eye of the lens was looking straight at them.

Then, haltingly, the web weaver began to stumble forward. Alice stared in horror at the smoking camera. The tripod legs were vibrating so hard and fast, they each seemed to split into two or three separate scuttling legs.

'Door!' shouted David, backing into Alice. Michael was nearest. His hands felt blindly for the handle and failed to find it.

'Quick!' begged Alice.

Michael touched the cold metal of the handle and tried to open the door, but his hand was slick with sweat and kept slipping. Then it was too late. The web weaver lurched forward and toppled towards them.

It nearly reached them. The lens bounced on to the carpet, centimetres from David's boot. He leapt out of the way as the camera gave one last shudder. The hissing shriek died away. The green light faded. The leather body shrivelled and flaked away from the frame and an oily black pool spread across the carpet.

'You did it,' breathed Michael.

'Doesn't look so big now, does it?' said Alice, grinning at David.

'There you are, Frankie,' said David, gazing out at the snow-filled sky. 'Does that feel better? Now all you have to do is keep going until we find you.'

'And what time did your friend leave the house?'

'She's called Frankie. Frankie Madigan,' said David.

'What time?' asked the sergeant.

'Some time in the last few hours,' said Alice.

The sergeant looked over the high desk at them. 'You don't know when?'

'She sneaked out!' said Alice. 'That's the point! She was – upset.'

'Ah. You had a row. She'll come back when she's cold enough.'

'Not from Cheildon,' said David. The sergeant raised her eyebrows, but David stared back determinedly.

'How do you know she's gone there? I can't imagine anyone going out for a hike in this weather. My guess is she's popped out to the shops. Maybe we should just hold on for a while before we go calling Border Search and Rescue –'

'She was upset,' blurted Alice. 'She was worried – about her parents. She thought – she thought they might be splitting up.'

'Ah,' said the Sergeant. 'But why Cheildon?'

David took a deep breath. 'She's been reading a book of Borderland stories. They were written by a man called Thomas Laidlaw who lived on Cheildon, hundreds of years ago –'

'Story books? This is a police station, not a library,' growled the sergeant.

'No, she's gone to Cheildon because she thinks she'll find the truth there. Please. You've got to believe us!'

The sergeant cleared her throat and picked up a pen. 'Description?'

David sighed with relief. 'She's black, with an American accent. She's small for her age –'

'Clothes?'

'Um,' David turned to Alice and Michael, who

101

both shrugged. 'Whatever she's wearing, it'll be different,' he said.

'Right.' The sergeant put her pen down and winked at Michael.

'So you'll call Border Rescue?' he asked.

'No. But I'll tell you what I will do. I'll put this description out locally and tell them to send her home if they spot her, all right?'

The sergeant's smile faded as she saw their faces.

'Where's the Border Rescue Base?' asked David in a tight voice.

'Cheildon Village,' said the sergeant, turning away to put her pen back. 'But I wouldn't advise you to travel anywhere now. There's a blizzard forecast.'

The door banged shut and the sergeant realised she was talking to an empty room. She frowned and moved to sit in front of a bank of television monitors. They were running a continual movie of the town centre, recorded by police cameras.

'Story books,' muttered the sergeant. She shook her head and selected a video of the main street. She began to view it on fast-forward, watching the Saturday shoppers zoom at impossible speeds up and down the street.

Suddenly she sat up straight and hit the pause button. There was a small black girl, frozen in the act of walking up to the bus station. She was wearing a big jacket, shorts and tiger-stripe tights and black Doc Marten boots.

'Hmmm. They're different enough. Nearly three hours ago,' said the sergeant, looking at the time on the film. 'Let's see where she's going.' The sergeant pressed the play button and watched Frankie climb on to a waiting bus. She moved the computer mouse to click the arrow on the front of the bus. The bus destination sign enlarged, filling the screen in big, black letters.

CHEILDON VILLAGE

'OK,' sighed the sergeant, swinging her chair round to face the radio. Her finger hovered over the switch for the Rescue Services frequency as she glanced out at the thickening snow.

'OK,' she repeated, flicking the switch and picking up the mike. 'Border Police to Border Search and Rescue. Come in, please . . .

By the time the bus crawled into Cheildon Village, the snow was blasting so hard against the windscreen, the wipers could not clear it. Drifts of snow were slowly taking over half the road and the other half was coated in ice.

'This is it,' said the driver. 'Cheildon Village.' He tried to stop at the bus shelter, but the bus slowly slid on to the pavement and buried its front end in a snowdrift.

Alice let out her breath. Her hands were hurting. She looked down and realised she had been clinging to her seat.

'Well,' said the driver in satisfaction, as he peered out at the bright windows of the pub, 'I think we can safely say I'm stranded.' He opened the doors and a howling wind blasted snow into the bus. 'You three got somewhere to go?' he asked, giving Alice, David and Michael a worried glance as they trooped to the front.

'Yes we do,' said Alice.

'We need to find the Border Search and Rescue Base,' said David. 'Do you know where it is?'

'I'll take you,' said a deep voice behind them. A man wearing a florescent green waistcoat climbed on to the bus and stamped the snow from his hiking boots. 'My name's Alex. Alex McGovern. I'm the team leader at Border Search and Rescue. And you must be Frankie's friends. We've been expecting you.'

Alex McGovern guided them through the blizzard to a tiny cottage with a tall radio mast attached to it. A four-wheel-drive vehicle was parked outside with a large trailer in tow. He opened the front door of the cottage and they walked into a room full of big men dressed in waterproof trousers and thick sweaters.

'But how did you know we were coming?' asked Michael, as soon as the door had shut out the noise of the blizzard.

'That sergeant you spoke to checked the police camera video after you'd gone and she saw your friend, Frankie, getting on the Cheildon Village bus. When she checked with the bus company, the driver remembered Frankie getting off here. No one's seen her since.'

Alice bit her lip and Alex McGovern put a large hand on her shoulder.

'Do her mum and dad know?' asked David.

'The police are trying to contact them. Now, can you tell us, is Frankie an experienced walker? Would she know what to do if she was caught in a blizzard?'

'No,' said David. The men glanced at one another over his head.

'The sergeant described her as – inadequately dressed. Would you agree?'

'Probably.'

Again the men glanced at one another and began moving quietly around them, lacing up hiking boots and pulling waterproof jackets over their sweaters.

'Would she be carrying any food or drink?' asked Alex McGovern.

'Look,' said David, swinging his head back and forth to watch the men. 'She was upset. She's gone up there with nothing.'

The radio burst into life and they all turned to watch the operator. 'The sergeant's got the parents with her at the police station,' he said, turning in his chair. 'They can't reach us here. The roads are blocked. Your bus was probably the last vehicle to get through,' he added, smiling at the children.

'General call out, please, James,' said Alex McGovern in a quiet voice. 'Get the search dogs out too.' The operator nodded and turned back to his radio.

'All right, boys,' continued the team leader. 'Ready to move? Blizzard conditions, I know, but we need to pull out all the stops on this one. Chris has been out with the plough for us, so we should be able to get the vehicle and trailer on to the lower slopes. We'll have a good three hours before dark, if we're lucky.'

The room cleared surprisingly quickly. Within two minutes, the only member of the rescue team left in the room was James, the radio operator. The children were left standing with their faces pressed against the Rescue Centre window, watching the flashing orange light of the rescue vehicle as it moved slowly away through the driving snow.

'OK, you three,' said James, guiding them over to a table. 'You sit here and I'll make you a cup of tea. Don't worry. They'll be back with Frankie before you know it.'

Silently, they gathered around the table. All they could think of was Frankie, up on the bare side of Cheildon in the blizzard.

10

Frankie climbed down from the bus in Cheildon Village. The snowy village square was deserted. She stared up at Cheildon Hill as it loomed behind the houses. There were five roads branching off from the square and, for a few seconds, Frankie could not decide which one to choose. She shook her head to clear it, but still it seemed full of a thick grey fog, stopping her from thinking straight. Then she spotted a signpost for walkers, pointing the way to Cheildon Hill.

Frankie set off at a determined pace, following the lane out of Cheildon Village and on to the lower slopes of Cheildon Hill. She could not get rid of the fuzzy feeling in her head. It made her feel as though she was still trapped in her room with the web weaver, even though she was miles away from home. Frankie wanted to climb to clearer air and escape the fog which surrounded her. She wanted to climb the side of Cheildon Hill and find the truth. Frankie swung her arms and planted her boots firmly in the snow.

For the first half an hour, the going was quite easy. There was a well-trodden footpath through the snow and the slope was not too steep. Frankie walked on, finding a rhythm, and finally she let herself think about the photograph. Her parents splitting up? She scowled ferociously. She could not bear the thought of losing either one of them. Her dad was kind and funny and gave her everything she wanted. Her mom was much stricter, which was a pain sometimes, but she was a good organiser and great at helping with homework. Frankie knew her mom would never let her down. She loved them both.

What if Alice, David and Michael were right? What if the camera was promising secrets but fooling her with tricks? They had been arguing a lot, her mom and dad, but did that mean they were going to split up? They had always argued, it was just that Frankie had never taken any notice of it before. She thought about the past week. Her parents had been together a lot. They still cooked like a team. They still finished one another's sentences. But the photograph . . . Frankie sighed and, once again, shook her head to clear it.

Suddenly, her boots slid out from under her and Frankie sat down very hard. The bump brought her back to the hillside with a jolt. She scrambled to her feet again and realised that she was out of breath. The slope had been gradually steepening without her noticing. She looked around her. There were no footsteps in the snow to follow now, in front of her or behind. She looked up. The slope ahead of her was much steeper. The ground was rough and uneven. In some places, the snow lay deep in hollows. In others, the wind had whipped the snow away, exposing slopes of slippery black scree. Frankie looked higher. She could not see the top of Cheildon Hill. It was hidden by dark grey clouds.

The cloud had moved in behind her too. The ground sloped away into grey mist. Frankie could not see the village, or even the well-trodden path on which she had started off. She stood, undecided, and her legs grew chilly as the snow from her fall soaked into her tights. A blast of icy wind caught her by surprise and she staggered.

The wind was growing stronger by the second and the sky was very dark. Frankie looked around anxiously. It struck her for the first time that it might be foolish to be out on the hill, alone, with the weather closing in. She thought about turning back, but the fog swirled in her head and she let the idea drift away. She bit her lip, wondering which way to go. Then the wind tore a hole in the cloud above her and she caught a glimpse of a ruined shepherd's bothy, high on the side of the hill.

That's where I'll go, she thought, as the snow began to tumble from the clouds. I'll keep climbing up to that hut. I can shelter there until the weather clears. She nodded, pleased with herself for making such a sensible decision. The icy wind was blasting snow across the hillside, and the bothy disappeared once more, but Frankie thought she knew the position of the little hut and she started to struggle towards it.

Soon her legs were so cold and wet, they began to

hurt. Her hands, without gloves, were just as bad, but Frankie dared not warm them in her jacket pockets. She had fallen twice more, once on a patch of icy snow and once when her foot had caught a hidden rock. Frankie needed her hands free in case she fell again.

The blizzard grew worse and worse. After a while there was nothing to see but a mass of swirling snow. The wind blasted the frozen particles into her face with such force she felt as though her skin was being scored away, strip by strip. She stumbled on, stopping more and more often to catch her breath and rub the crusted snow from her eyebrows and lashes.

When the ground gave way beneath her feet, Frankie tried to scream, but her mouth filled up with snow. She had fallen into a deep drift, caught in a hollow on the hillside. Frankie panicked. She floundered in the powdery snow, feeling it pack itself ever more solidly around her legs, until her hand scraped against a rock. She grabbed the rock and hauled herself slowly out of the drift and back on to solid ground.

She knelt there for a time, sobbing with exhaustion. The snow from the drift had packed in under her jacket and was melting against her skin, taking the last warmth away from her. Frankie rubbed at her face with the back of her hands, trying to bring some feeling back to her numb cheeks, but it was no good. Her face felt like a frozen mask. She raised her head and peered at the walls of swirling snow all around her and realised she no longer knew which way to go. Fear settled on her shoulders.

Turn back, she thought, but again the fog filled her head and the idea was lost. No, I've got to go up, she decided. That's the only way. I've got to find that little hut and get some shelter from the wind. Otherwise I might . . .

Frankie struggled to her feet, refusing to finish the last thought. It was only a hill! Hills weren't dangerous, were they? Mountains, yes. People died on mountains, but not on hills! Turn back, she thought, and again the fog blanketed her mind. Frankie put her hands to her head and realised that her hat was gone, taken by the wind. Suddenly she heard her mother's voice.

'Always wear a hat in cold weather, Frances. You lose a third of your body heat through your head.'

'OK, Mom,' she panted, looping a length of scarf over her head. It took her three attempts to tie the scarf under her chin, but finally she managed it. 'There you go, Mom. Hat on. I'm safe now. Nothing can get me now.' Frankie giggled and the giggle turned into a whimper. She clenched her teeth and forced her legs to start moving again.

The snow danced in front of her eyes and the fog swirled in her head. Frankie reeled off-course, moving crabwise over to the right. Again and again, she altered her direction, turning back to climb the slope towards the bothy, then dizzily veering off to the right. Ahead of her, barely six steps away, the glassy black surface of a scree slope waited.

Frankie stumbled a few more steps sideways, head down, then jerked to a halt. Her eyes grew wide. The fog in her head had suddenly lifted away as cleanly as a curtain. Frankie gasped. The web weaver had gone! Her mind was sharp and clear and – she smiled – Ian Elliot was her friend again and her parents . . . Frankie stopped smiling. She still did not know the answer to that question.

Frankie turned away from the scree slope without realising how close she was. She began to climb straight up the hill once more, parallel to the scree. She nearly cleared it. Then a blast of wind knocked her sideways and suddenly she was scrambling on the icy top edge of the slope.

Her boots slid and skittered on the glassy surface. She fell hard against the shale, scrabbling for a handhold. The slope began to move beneath her as each individual shard of stone broke free from the ice which held it there. Frankie screamed as she began to slide. She tried to grip with numb fingers and dug her toes into the shale. Slivers of stone clattered and bounced down the slope all around her and she knew she would soon follow, sliding and crashing down the slick, black ice, picking up speed all the way until she hit the rocks at the bottom.

'Here.'

Frankie looked up and saw a stout stick within reach of her left hand. She grabbed the stick and held on tight.

'Now your other hand.'

Frankie could not find the courage to make her

right hand let go of the frozen scree and reach over to the stick.

'I can't!'

'Look at me.'

The voice was firm. Frankie raised her head once more and thought she saw the brightest blue eyes, looking down at her. She let go of the scree and grabbed the stick. Her boots slid from the slope and Frankie was left hanging over the drop. She hauled herself up with the last of her strength and fell into the snow at the top edge of the scree slope.

'I found you!' she sobbed.

'I have been here all along,' said the voice. 'Only you could not see me until now.'

For a time, Frankie lay still, gasping for breath. Then, once again, she clambered to her feet.

She stood swaying in the wind. There was no sign of the stout stick she had grasped so desperately and already the memory of the bright blue eyes was fading. She moved away from the treacherous slope, then stopped and sat down. She no longer felt cold. The snow looked soft and welcoming. Frankie decided to lie down, just for a little while, before she moved on.

Her eyes were closing when she saw the light ahead of her. It was a warm, orange light. It flickered through the snow. Frankie left her soft, white bed reluctantly and crawled towards the light. As she got closer, she saw that the light was a fire and the fire was burning in the fireplace of a little stone hut.

Frankie climbed to her feet and staggered to the

open door of the bothy. In she went, into the warm room and up to the fire. Frankie curled up into a ball in front of the fire and fell asleep. Outside, the wind slowly lost power. The falling snow thinned out and stopped. The cloud cleared from the sky and the temperature began to drop.

Alex McGovern looked up at the darkening sky and then at his Rescue Team, spread out across the hill for a line search. On the slope above them, the dog handler worked his search dog, encouraging her to find any trace of human scent on the air. They had been on the side of Cheildon for nearly three hours and they had found no sign of the girl. The blizzard had cleared but night was coming in fast.

'Over here!'

Alex looked up the slope. The dog handler was pointing at his collie dog who was sniffing excitedly at the bottom of a steep scree slope. His heart sank. If she had fallen down there, then there was not much hope.

'Reiver Control to Reiver One. Say again?' said the radio operator in the Border Rescue building. The radio squawked and he pressed his finger to the earpiece. David, Alice and Michael gathered around, waiting.

'Reiver Control to Reiver One. All received,' said the radio operator. He turned in his chair. 'They've found her scarf at the bottom of a scree slope.

No sign of her yet. They're going to carry on the search.'

The children turned despondently and went back to the window to stare at the great white bulk of Cheildon, towering over the village.

The rescue team quartered the area around the scree slope, searching every hollow, but they found nothing. Alex McGovern cupped his hands to his mouth. 'Frankie! Can you hear us? Frankie!'

There was no reply. Alex McGovern sighed. He had not really been expecting one. The girl had been out for hours in a blizzard, without any protection, and the temperature was dropping. The wind-chill factor alone would have caused severe hypothermia by now. He guessed that Frankie was lying somewhere on the side of Cheildon, deeply unconscious. But where?

He scanned the hillside, trying to decide whether to move up or across. The blizzard had covered any possible footprints. He tried to work out what Frankie might have done. If the scarf was at the bottom of the scree slope, then maybe she had been moving across the hill instead of climbing? Alex McGovern looked up at the steep hillside and decided that Frankie would have followed the path of least resistance. He decided to move the search sideways, over to the right.

'Reiver One to Reiver Control,' he said into his radio. 'Our new position will be due west . . .' He stopped halfway through the message and stared at

115

the hillside directly above him. A warm orange light was winking through the dusk. The others were pointing too.

'Where's that come from?'

'Looks like a fire.'

'That's the old bothy, isn't it?'

Alex McGovern smiled. 'Reiver One to Reiver Control. Cancel that information. Our new position will be the old bothy. We've just spotted a light. Repeat, we have spotted a light.'

There was no light when they reached the ruined bothy, only a piece of Frankie's red jacket, bright against the snow. Alex McGovern bent and swept the snow from around the jacket and a mass of black hair came into view. Gently, he lifted the hair from Frankie's face and her eyelids fluttered. He straightened up and reached for his radio.

'Reiver One to Reiver Control. We've found her,' he said. 'We're bringing her down.'

'Here it is!' called David as the Rescue Vehicle and trailer drove slowly down the street. Alice and Michael hugged one another. James hurried out to meet the team, but the children hung back, waiting. Frankie had been found alive, that was all they knew. They preferred to watch from the window.

Gently, Alex McGovern passed a padded sleeping bag down to James.

'She must be in there,' said Alice.

James turned and walked carefully back to the building, carrying Frankie.

'She must be all right,' said Michael, rushing to open the door. 'Look. He's smiling.'

'She's OK,' called James, hurrying into the room. Carefully he put the bundle down on a chair and unzipped the sleeping bag. Frankie emerged from the fleece-lined interior, looking warm and sleepy.

'Oh, Frankie,' said Alice, and her eyes filled with tears. Michael and David grinned and nudged one another in relief as the rescue team came in and stood around Frankie, staring at her as though she had two heads.

'I don't understand it,' said Alex McGovern, frowning down at Frankie as the doctor bent over her. 'She should have been deeply hypothermic after all that time in freezing temperatures, but she was as warm as toast when we found her in that ruined bothy. The only sign of hypothermia was the hallucinations. She was delirious when we woke her. She kept asking why we'd let the fire go out and where had the roof gone.' He shook his head. 'That bothy hasn't seen a roof in a long time. What do you think, doc? Can you explain it?'

The doctor finished his examination and stood back. 'The covering of snow could've kept her warm,' he said. 'Or maybe . . . I've known some kids use a sort of shut-down facility in order to survive extreme conditions. Maybe she did that.' He shrugged. 'I don't know what happened, to be honest. She's suffering from slight exposure and just a few cuts and bruises. I'll patch her up and then you can give her some soup if you like.'

The rescue team moved away to strip off their outer clothes, still shaking their heads.

'Frankie?' whispered Alice, moving close.

'Hi, guys,' said Frankie, lifting her heavy eyelids.

'Are you OK?' asked Michael.

'Yeah. I'm fine. He looked after me.'

'Who did?' said David.

'The Truth Teller,' said Frankie.

David raised his eyebrows and folded his arms. 'Mr McGovern was right. She's delirious.'

'We're so glad to have you back,' said Alice, frowning at David. 'You – you are really back, aren't you?'

'What do you mean?' muttered Frankie, closing her eyes.

'David zapped the web weaver with a mirror,' said Michael. 'It was amazing!'

Frankie smiled. 'I knew that,' she said simply. 'Thanks, Davey.'

'Is it really over?' whispered Michael.

They leaned forward, waiting for an answer, but Frankie sighed tiredly and let her head fall back against the chair.

'You'll need to move away for a while,' said the doctor, coming back with his bag. 'This young lady's mum and dad are here to see her. It's time for them to be together.'

Frankie smiled. 'Mom *and* dad,' he'd said. It sounded good. Reluctantly, Michael, Alice and David began to back off.

'Hey, Alice,' called Frankie, raising her head to

peer past the doctor, 'I wish you wouldn't keep wearing that top. How many times have I told you the colour's too dark for you?'

Alice smiled, and so did the others. First David and then, more slowly, Michael.

Frankie was back now – for sure.